A Grave on
Deacon's Peak

Unsettling Accounts

A Grave on Deacon's Peak

By

Bryan
Babel

**DARK
TIDINGS**
P R E S S

A Grave on Deacon's Peak is a work of fiction. Names, characters, places, and incidents are the products of the author's imagination or are used fictitiously. Any resemblance to actual events, locales, or persons, living or dead, is entirely coincidental.

Cover art by Cristina Tanase

Hardcover ISBN: 978-1-951138-00-4
Paperback ISBN: 978-1-951138-01-1
eBook ISBN: 978-1-951138-02-8

First Edition, July 2019

Dark Tidings Press LLC
PO Box 593
Albany, OR 97321

darktidingspress.com

To my brother, John. For Courage and Encouragement.

A Grave on Deacon's Peak

Chapter One:
A Long Row To Hoe

My name is Bob Bellamy, and in the year 1803, when I was twelve years old, I had the most peculiar adventure you ever heard of. This is how it began.

We sat in the lawyer's office in New York, Mother and I, and listened to him talk on and on. The afternoon sunlight picked out the gold lettering on the law books piled on his shelves, and the scent of leather ledgers and fresh parchment spiced the air. Mr. Frobisher-the lawyer, that is—had obvious political ambitions and never let one word serve when five would do. The plain upshot was that Father was gone, nobody knew whither, and must be considered dead.

"There you have it, Mrs. Bellamy." Mr. Frobisher sat back his long body, his lantern jaw sinking into his collar, and his hands sliding under his wide lapels. "A most unfortunate circumstance for the government, as well as yourself and your family. A patriot, a tried and true servant of his country, doing service on an important mission, which I am, alas, unable to reveal even now to you. A mission with such an element of danger that we must presume after this length of time that he has nobly sacrificed his life in its pursuit."

"You mean you think he is dead," said Mother.

The lawyer put his hand up as if in protest.

"So harsh a term…" he began.

"You need not think to spare my feelings, sir. As his wife, I believe I am more nearly concerned than you, and I have used the term. You will find I am not the kind of person to easily presume the death of a loved one. In fact, until I see a gravestone, I shall continue to hope for his return. But as the mother of his children-"—here she nodded at me—"-I cannot afford to wait or go beating about the bush. What about the money?"

The lawyer's eyebrows shot up to the line of his powdered wig.

"Money, Mrs. Bellamy?"

"The money, Mr. Frobisher," my Mother said firmly. "Promised to my husband in pension to his family in the case of his demise. As a tried and true servant of his country." She reached into her bag and drew out a paper heavy with seals and signatures. "This is his copy of the original contract."

Mr. Frobisher took the paper and read it, rubbing his finger back and forth along his jaw. He shook his head and handed it back.

"You must realize, my dear lady, the problems the present government faces. The fact that Mr. Bellamy cannot be proved dead means that we cannot, at this time, honor the agreement, as he may actually be alive."

"But if you proceed on the assumption he *is* alive, then he still must be pursuing your interests on this mission and you must continue paying his wages into our account until he returns or is proved to be deceased."

"Alas, no, madam. The situation as it is means he must be presumed dead, or worse, malfeasant, in which case all contracts and agreements would be rendered null and void, and his character, ahem, would suffer detrimentally."

"You mean he would be branded a traitor."

"As you say. In the meantime, I fear seven years must pass before the law can consider him safely dead, and by then—"

"By then you will be out of office, and it will be the next government's responsibility. If they will even honor the contract." Mother replaced the paper calmly and carefully, but I noticed a slight trembling in her hands, which I knew to be a sign of controlled anger, not fear. She rose to her feet and stood straight, her eyes flashing.

"Very well. The grateful nation presumes its agent dead, and has nothing for the presumed widow, or the presumed orphans. We shall go and make our way as best we can. You may feel, Mr. Frobisher, that legally you are absolved in this case, but you will find that morally you are far from quits in the matter, and that there is a higher Bench of Appeal than the Supreme Court. Let us take our leave, Robert."

Yes, my mother called me Robert in public, in her formal way, instead of plain Bob. She was from Boston. We knew that Boston was the best and most cultured city in Massachusetts, and Massachusetts the finest state in the Union, and the United States the greatest country in the world. And to our father, who was born in Virginia, and to ourselves—that is, to me and my sister, Daisy—our mother was plainly the finest flower

Boston had ever produced. I stood up as straight as I could to match the dignity of her tone and cast on Mr. Frobisher a scornful glare.

"My dear lady." The lawyer jack-knifed himself to his feet. "My dear lady, do not be so hasty. I did not mean that there was nothing that could be done in your case. I feel greatly for your plight—believe me I do." The wattle was quivering back and forth on his collar, and I could see he was moved, but whether by sympathy or apprehension it was hard to tell. He gestured back at our seats.

Mother sat primly down in her chair, never taking her eyes off the lawyer, rather as if he were a large dog she did not entirely trust.

"Well?" she asked. "What can be done?"

Mr. Frobisher sat back in his chair and brushed his forehead with his left hand, knocking the desk with the knuckles of his right fist as if counting or calculating. Finally, he cleared his throat and leaned forward.

"I can pay you half his wages for this last month. That is the most I feel I can safely extend to you in the country's name. Yes, I know that is not much," he held up a hand to forestall my mother's rising protest. "However, in view of your circumstances, I am also willing to help you personally, out of my own charity."

"I hope you will do me the honor of realizing that I did not come to you for charity but for my rights."

"Believe me, Mrs. Bellamy, I would not offer it to you if I did not think you in some respects deserved it, in place of your deferred honorarium. There are also, as you say, the children to be considered, who should not be sacrificed on the altar of your pride, no matter how justified. Ahem—there is a certain grace to receiving as well as offering charity, you know."

Mother seemed to unbend a shade. She nodded her head.

"You are quite right, Mr. Frobisher, and I thank you for reminding me of it. You have also brought to bear the one argument I cannot refuse, the welfare of my children. Very well. What is the nature of this charity you propose to extend us?"

"It is this, madam." He rummaged in his desk drawer a moment and pulled out a folder closed with a button and a string. He began to unwind the string from around the button.

"Some months ago, it fell to my duty to wind up the affairs of a man who passed away on his holding outside a small frontier village without lawyer, will, or heir—an untidy proceeding, which I advise you to avoid. An heir is not totally necessary, and may be dispensed with, but to die without a lawyer or a will is thoughtless in the extreme. Aha."

He finished unwinding the string and opened the folder.

"In any case, his land and house came into my management, and it has become my duty to dispose of them in some manner. It was my first instinct to rent the place out, but local opinion has formed some sort of prejudice against it, and that has proved impossible. The absence of a tenant has been debilitating to the property—"

"You mean since no-one has lived there it has been running down."

"Precisely. This, of course, is making it ever harder and harder to find a paying tenant, and local opinion, being of a rustic and uneducated nature, has formed certain superstitious prejudices about the property, which I feel the presence of a family, especially one headed by a pragmatic and high-spirited lady such as yourself, would go far to disperse."

Mother frowned. "Superstitious prejudices?"

The lawyer waved his hand dismissively. "The usual thing. The deceased owner—a Deacon Whitley—was a reclusive and rather eccentric fellow. Foolish tales of ha'nts and mysterious lights are *de rigueur* when such hermits pass away, along with stories of buried hoards of treasure. Stories that I looked into myself, and which I can assure you are totally unfounded."

My ears pricked up. Buried treasure! If that were true, and I managed to find it, our money worries would be over. That old devil Frobisher might have nosed around the place, but he didn't seem half as clever as I could be when I was investigating things. I looked sidelong at Mother, silently wishing her to accept the lawyer's offer.

I did not have long to wait. "Very well," said Mother. "We are not wholly accustomed to country living, but needs must, I always say, and I am not afraid of hard work. Until such time as my husband returns—or until you find some paying customer, I am sure—we shall live on and take care of the Whitley property."

"Excellent, Mrs. Bellamy!" The lawyer screwed his face into an approximation of congeniality. "Allow me to draw up a few papers and a letter of introduction and get your money, and we can conclude our business. Fall nears apace, and I am sure there are many things you will want to prepare before winter. I suggest you make no delays."

"I am not of a delaying nature, Mr. Frobisher."

"Indeed not, Mrs. Bellamy."

For all their talk of speed, my mother and the lawyer were not totally done with things for a good round hour, during which I fidgeted and tried to amuse myself, without much success. The only interesting moment was when the old man opened an enormous cast-iron safe to draw forth a woefully small bag of coins—the last of Father's wages we would see for a long while—which he gave to Mother. It was well into dinnertime when we finally stood on the porch of Mr. Frobisher's law offices, and he bowed over Mother's hand in farewell.

"Adieu, madam. I wish you every good fortune in your new endeavors." There was a twinkle in his eye. "I will venture to prophesy, on the strength of our short acquaintance, that any ghosts or redskins you may encounter in the wild will meet more than their match in you."

"You mean, sir, that you find me a little more terrifying than either." Mother could barely suppress her smile of pride and amusement. "Good day, Mr. Frobisher."

We stepped out into the muddy street and began walking north.

"Are we going to the oyster bar, Ma?" I asked. "I'm surely hungry."

"No, first we are going to Mrs. Gurton's to pick up your sister. And then we are going to get some bread and cheese and eat in the boarding house. Meals at restaurants are out of the question for a while."

"Yes, Ma," I said meekly and nudged a pig out of the way with my foot. New York was already a big city at the time, but uncontrolled pigs still wandered the neighborhoods and made walking a very adventurous activity. "Ma, do you think Pa is dead?"

We walked silently on a bit.

"I do not *know* that he is dead," she finally answered. "Therefore, we may hope he is alive. But in the meanwhile, we must act and plan as if we are on our own. I'm afraid it will be a rather long row to hoe. And that means more economies we have to practice. We will leave the hotel, sell what we don't need, and travel immediately to the Whitley Farm. Our motto must be the old saw: use it up, wear it out, make it do or do without."

There was a look of grim satisfaction on Mother's face. I knew that look. Father never tired of telling us the tale of how when he asked for her hand. He, a poor fellow with no family and no prospects. Grandmother Morrison had looked down her nose at him and said, in effect, that her daughter was something of a hothouse flower and that she could never flourish in common dirt. Mother set out there and then to prove she was no fading lily, and the first way she did it was to marry Father in spite of her family's protests.

It was with almost military pride that we marched through the streets until we came to Mrs. Gurton's Nursery Academy, a small green building surrounded by a yard with trees and a white picket fence. As we made our way up the walk to the front entrance, we became aware of a great hullabaloo of noise from inside.

"What in the world?" said Mother as she turned the knob and revealed to our wondering eyes the scene of chaos within.

Inside the usually strictly regimented classroom, someone had constructed a towering fortress from desks, grammar books, and tuck-boxes. Children from tiny toddlers to big seven years old were milling around it, screaming, yelling, and talking excitedly, some in fear, some in delight. Several determined young boys were making an effort to climb the structure, with little success. For astride the top of the piled desks, her face beet red but triumphant, and her ponytails sticking straight up like the Devil's own horns, was my six-year-old sister, Daisy.

In her hands was the teacher's much used and well-seasoned hickory stick.

"Here I am, the king of the castle," she sing-songed. One of the climbers got too close, reaching out his hand to grab her leg. "Get you *gone*," she cried, bringing down the stick with an almighty *crack* next to his hands, and he jumped down with a frightened yelp. "You dirty rascal!" she completed the rhyme happily.

"Mrs. Bellamy! Thank goodness you've come!" Mrs. Gurton had spotted us and was hurrying over, her flabby jowls flapping in outrage. "We returned from the noon break and found her like this. Look what she did when I tried to get her down!"

The teacher held out one of her tough, fleshy claws. A red stripe pulsed painfully across the knuckles.

"That child is out of control!" she hissed.

"We shall see," said Mother calmly. She turned to the piled desks where my sister was still occupied with fending off her besiegers. "Daisy!"

Daisy looked up, noticing us for the first time. She smiled. "Hello, Ma!" she cried cheerfully.

Mother held out her arms. "Come down to me, child."

Without hesitation, my sister dropped the hazel stick and leaped the two yards over into my mother's waiting grasp. Mother straightened with her in her arms, and Daisy gave her a happy kiss on the cheek. "That's a good girl," she said.

As Mother put her down on her own feet again, Mrs. Gurton, having hastily recovered her rod of office, stalked over with murder in her eyes.

"Now I've got you, you little devil..." The old woman pulled back one of the sleeves of her dark green dress in preparation for chastisement, revealing a wrinkled but ham-like forearm.

"I'll teach you to strike your teacher."

"Restrain yourself, Mrs. Gurton," said Mother evenly. "You must remember the power of an instructor such as yourself to punish a child is received in the parent's absence, to act as a guardian as they would and protect them as such. Well, I am here, and the duty reverts to me. If there is to be any correction, I shall do it."

"If?" Mrs. Gurton sputtered, and would have said more, but Mother had already turned to my sister and bent down to speak to her.

"Now, Daisy, what is this all about?"

"It started this mornin'," she said. "Mrs. Gurton gave me a swat on my hand. She said I was talkin', but I wasn't. Then she switched me two more times for nothin'."

"The child thinks she'd too good to be switched!" Mrs. Gurton sneered, working her face into a pucker of disdain. "She won't be corrected!"

"It wasn't being switched," said Daisy, looking at the old lady with contempt. "My Daddy switches harder than you. It was you was unfair."

"Life is unfair, young lady."

"Life is an abstract concept, Mrs. Gurton," my mother replied. "We, as moral beings, must adhere to a higher standard. Why do you think, Daisy, that Mrs. Gurton was so unfair?"

This was a good question. I knew Daisy was something of a pet with the old lady, as she already knew how to read and write before she got to the Academy, didn't have to be taught, and was sometimes singled out with pride as one of Mrs. Gurton's *successes*, although the teacher had little to do with it.

"We-e-ell," Daisy drawled, "I think she heard me tellin' my

friend Theodora that she dyes her hair with tea leaves."

"Oh!" The old teacher gasped. Every eye in the room was suddenly fixed on her hair, from the curious gaze of the three-year-olds to my mother's assessing stare. It *was* the light brown color of old tea, except at the roots where it was iron gray. In the sudden stillness of the room, I swear I could smell it, like a stale cup left overnight.

"I `membered what Daddy said about resistin' injustice," Daisy continued. "So, at lunch I built a fort and got a weapon to defend myself till you came to take me home. I did give Mrs. Gurton a smack when she tried to get me, but she smacked me first, and wrongly. After that, she ordered the boys to try to pull me down. Daddy's right about tyrants bein' cowards," she added philosophically.

"You wicked girl!" Mrs. Gurton shrieked. She was shaking with wrath and embarrassment, and between the two of them, I thought she was about to have a fit. "Mrs. Bellamy, I will not have that child in my school! I'm expelling her, do you hear me? She is never to come here again. She is banned from the Academy, and she will receive no certificate of accomplishment."

There were little cries of dismay from the school children, especially loud from Theodora, my sister's best friend. The certificate of accomplishment was the carrot held in front of them, and to threaten its loss was one of the old lady's prime methods of motivation. Mother simply narrowed her eyes a little. I stepped back a ways, in case of danger.

But she was calm. "That's just as well," she said. "I came early today to tell you we are leaving and have to withdraw Daisy. I must confess I enrolled her here for the company she would have of other children. I was a little worried she would not wish to leave, but I can see the parting will be a happy one for both of you. Get your things, dear, and prepare to go. Your principles are sound, my child, but your methods might be considered a little radical."

"Yes, Mama." She turned and meekly began to gather her things.

The old pedagogue was beside herself.

"What! Aren't you going to punish her?"

"No, I don't think so. And if I were you, madam, I would not bring up the subject of punishment, lest I find it personally applied. A place like this thrives on its reputation, and nothing that happened here today would help yours. I think you will be lucky if the only outcome will be that your students' parents know about your hair, which is, after all, only a foible and not a sin. Come, children, let us go."

Mrs. Gurton looked at Mother and went pale, then gathered herself and turned to the class.

"Put those desks back in place!" she bawled. "Get this room in order. We still have lessons to learn." She turned to Mother. "Good day, Mrs. Bellamy. I will not keep you."

Mother gave a small, humorous nod of acknowledgement, and we all left. The old lady followed us and stood in the doorway, watching us go with a scowl on her face. As we turned to shut the gate, Daisy saw the sad figure of her friend, Theodora, standing in the teacher's shadow, waving after us with tears in her eyes.

"Don't worry, Thea!" Daisy cried, waving back. "We'll meet again, I know it. I'll write you! Until then, Death to All Tyrants!"

Mrs. Gurton looked scandalized and slammed the door. Daisy smiled contentedly to herself, then looked up to Mother.

"Now, where are we goin'?"

Chapter Two:
Up A Crooked Path

"Madam, have you no friends? No one to warn you off this rash enterprise?"

For three days in New York, we had been in and out of pawn shops and second-hand stores, selling what little we could spare and buying articles we knew we would need. Now we were in the little town of Cumberton, to purchase flour and molasses and gunpowder and other such staples. All had been calculated to a nicety and was not a totally unfamiliar process to our family, as Father had often relocated us where his job took him.

Nowadays, when people think of the frontier, they think of grassy plains and covered wagons and dusty heat. But we were now in the north, rumbling through dark woods, hilly countryside, and cold rolling waters. Ten days by coach had left us weary but unbowed in this tiny valley town in the Northwest Territory, the closest to the deserted house at the foot of the mountains. The proprietor of the trading post looked at Mother with an assessing, squinted eye.

"Mr. Culpepper, even if I had any such friends who would discourage me so, I would have little choice to heed them. This should cover our purchases, with a little to spare." She placed a five-dollar gold piece with a snap on the counter. I looked at it longingly. It was by far the largest piece of money we had.

"Now, is there any service that can take us up into the hills?"

Mr. Amos Culpepper sucked in his breath and pursed his lips. His fingers played on the counter like a drum as he rolled an eye over the shop. It was low and dark, crammed with boxes and barrels, but impeccably clean. For a moment, he seemed to be lost in contemplation of the cured hams and strings of onions that hung festooned from the rafters. He snapped back to earth.

"I can take you myself. I don't know as anybody else will drop by today." He pulled a cash box from under the counter, scooped the gold piece in, and began rattling around for change.

"How much—" Mother began, but he held up a forestalling hand, and gave her the handful of copper she had left.

"Consider it a welcome to Cumberton and a service of Culpepper's Trading Post, ma'am." He put the box away, then stood up, both hands on the counter. Although he must have been a tall man at one time, his back seemed bent in a permanent stoop. "If your boy can help me hitch up the mare, we can get to the Deacon's place with some daylight to spare."

"That's most kind of you, Mr. Culpepper. Thank you very much," Mother said, bowing her head. "Robert, assist the gentleman with his horse."

"Yes, Mother."

Mr. Culpepper picked up a knobby walking stick. We left Mother and Daisy behind, my sister curiously examining the bits and bobs in the lower shelves. He led me out back, where a steady square brown mare was cropping the grass in the paddock. The moment she noticed us, she trotted up obediently. The old man smiled as she lowered her head to his affectionate hand. We took her out and hitched her up to the flat wagon parked under the lean-to next the shop.

"Can you drive, boy?" He turned and looked down at me, a little sternly. I felt like I was being tested.

I hesitated.

"I'm learning, sir. My Pa was teaching me."

"You say so? Let's see you take us up to the front door."

He jumped into the seat, almost as if he were on springs despite his bowed back, and gave me a hand up. He unwrapped the reins and handed them over, then looked at me expectantly. I pulled the leather in, adjusting it to my reach.

"Gee," I said, and gave a little shake.

I was lucky the mare was so docile. I could feel her strength quivering through the tackle, pulling the body of the wagon into motion. With the lightest hand, I turned us into the road and up to the face of the shop, where Ma and Daisy were already waiting and watching under the overhang. With a "Whoa," I brought the wagon to a halt, with the tail just lined up to the front step.

"Good lad," he said. "Nicely done. What's your name again, boy?"

"Bob, sir."

"Well, Bob, let me show you how to load a wagon."

We began with the luggage where it sat piled under the eaves. It went in the front of the flatbed, the big trunk in the middle, and the smaller bags on either side.

"Your Ma and Sissy can ride on that. The supplies go over the rear axle. The weight makes it easier to steer."

"Where should I ride?"

"You can ride up with me, on the buckboard." I couldn't actually see his mouth because of his enormous white mustache, but the rest of his face wrinkled into a smile. "You might need a few lessons on driving in the hills, I reckon."

We went back into the store, where Daisy and Mother had already retired. An intense discussion was in progress. I wouldn't like to call it an argument, because Daisy would never have the temerity to argue with Mother, but it certainly was a debate as closely argued as any you could hear at town hall.

"It is an extravagance, dear," said Mother.

"We don't know that unless we ask the man the price," said Daisy.

"It is not necessary, my child."

"It could have lots of uses."

"It is a piece of gimcrackery."

"But it's nice, and I like it. Please, Ma? Just ask the price?"

"Well, what's going on here?" asked the old man. His eyes glinted slyly under his wrinkled brow. "A sour note in the family harmony? What's the to-do?"

"Daisy has found something she would like me to purchase." Mother's voice was stern, her lips pressed thin. "I think she wants it because it looks like a toy."

"It's not a toy." Daisy stamped her foot. Her pigtails went flying around her shoulders with the force of it. "It's dead useful, and I like the look of it."

"Well, let's just see it, my little lady," said Culpepper.

Daisy trotted over to a lower shelf in the far-left corner and came back clutching a tin barrel with both hands. It looked like it might hold a pint. It was shaped like a bee-hive, and the handle of the lid was a bee, with outspread wings.

"Here," she said. "What's that worth?"

Mr. Culpepper took the tin from her hands and examined it, turning it this way and that.

"Almost forgot I had these. Bought `em—ten?, twelve years ago? Haven't sold one in a donkey's age. This is the last one left. Little shopworn now." He dusted a quick, rasping hand over the lid. Motes fell to the floor. "Needs a bit of a shine. A touch of care."

He set the barrel on the counter briskly.

"When I got these, they were going for five cents," he announced.

Daisy's face fell.

"I only get a penny allowance a month." Her mouth quivered. "Somebody might buy it before I get enough saved up!"

"As I was going to say," Culpepper went on gravely, bending down to address Daisy directly. "In the condition it's in, it could sit on the shelf till Doomsday and I'd never sell it at that price. So, to make a little of my money back and free up some stock space…it's a penny to you, little lady." He looked up at Ma. "If that's fine with you, Ma'am."

Ma looked relieved.

"That would be most satisfactory, Mr. Culpepper. Your kindnesses abound." She fished a penny out of her bag. He slipped it into his pocket, then took the barrel and courteously presented it to Daisy.

"There you are. The lid opens with a twist to the left

and closes with a twist to the right. No varmints will get into that."

"We can put cookies into it," said Daisy. "Or nuts, or if we find some honey, or…well, lots of things."

"You must get the most enjoyment out of it as you can," said Mother. "I have to tell you, children, there will be no allowances from now on for perhaps quite a while."

I must have made some kind of noise, because everybody suddenly looked up at me. It seemed kind of hard that Daisy got one last present and I got nothing. I quickly turned the noise into a sneeze, but I don't think I fooled anybody.

"You can hang onto that," Mr. Culpepper said. "I'll get the rest of your purchases loaded up."

He led Mother and Daisy out to the wagon and helped them in, then began lugging the supplies into the back. I took it upon myself to help him as much as I could. After the last sack had been stacked, and the tailgate secured, we went back in one last time. He threw a faded blue coat on and a battered, tricorne hat. Only the right side of the hat was still up. As he put it on, I noticed he was wearing the back of his hair in a peruke, a little bundle like a pigtail. Father had pointed one out to me once and said almost no one wore them now.

He locked the store, and we clattered down the steps to the cart.

"All set back there? Everybody best keep their eyes peeled so you'll know the way again." He climbed back into the seat and helped me up. "That goes double for you, boy. I expect you'll be the one going up and down the mountain running errands. The road crooks back and forth at an easy slope for horses, but if you know where to look, there's a path straight down if you're on foot and in a real hurry. Gee up, Marybelle!"

The wagon lurched gently into motion, and we were on our way. At first, we passed through Cumberton itself, which didn't take long. There were about thirty houses. Mr. Culpepper called our attention to a few as we passed.

"There on the right, that's the smithy. Young Abner works it. Probably need to take anything that's broke over there. Carpenter right next him, Jehu Barsett, good feller if you want re-shingling done on old Deacon's house, which I don't doubt. There on the left lives Mrs. Struyken, our midwife. Closest thing we have to a doctor, yet. You can see the church spire from here—`Piscopalian—and Parson Word lives right against it."

Then we were out of town but still travelling along the coach road. About a half mile later, we turned into another way on our right and began taking the long, gentle slope doglegging into the hills. I looked up. The bare peak of the mountain rose out of the tangled trees and climbed to the sky. It neither welcomed or threatened but gazed indifferently down as we started to crawl up its knees, like insects. I felt like it might notice us eventually, and then possibly crush us for our impudence. I shuddered and looked down.

"Mr. Culpepper."

"Aye, lad?"

"This Deacon Whitley. What was he like?"

"Ah. Jerimoth Whitley."

He drove on silently. There was only the jingle of the harness and the crush of the wheels for a moment. A hawk screamed from the deep pines that grew on either side of us.

"He weren't really a deacon, you know. People just called him that from the way he dressed. He always carried around a black book, but the few people who ever got a look in it said it was no kind of Bible they ever saw. You folks got a Bible?"

"We do. And Shakespeare's Works, and an almanac. They were…they're my Pa's."

"Good lad. That makes you the next best library in town, after the parson." We jingled along. "Anyways, best keep your Bible handy while you're at the Whitley place. And always say your prayers."

"Why?"

Mr. Culpepper looked around the trees, at the road, and at last up at the sky. But not at me.

"It's always a good thing to say your prayers, boy. And to read the good book. Why not?" He shifted and settled back, looking away.

I studied him. He held himself stiffly, and his expression was bland. But I noticed his eyes every now and then, darting at the sun, as if to gauge the remaining light. I let him be for a bit, but kept inspecting him. Something dangling from his coat on the left lapel caught my eye.

"Is that a medal? Were you in the war?"

"I was in a lot of wars," he said. "But this ain't no medal. The only thing I brought out of my fighting days was a bullet in my bones that won't let me stand up straight." He shifted the reins into one hand and patted the glinting round disc bouncing at his chest.

"This, Mister Bob, is to commemorate the great General George Washington, who I had the honor to see and serve in the War of Independence. This was struck on the occasion of his passing, so we would never forget him. As if we ever could."

"You knew President Washington?" My eyes were round. Everybody knew of George Washington. But to meet someone who had seen him was like meeting someone who had witnessed

Moses coming down from the mountain with the Ten Commandments. I squirmed in my seat, sudden interest in the old man renewed. "What was he like?"

Culpepper chuckled.

"I don't know what *President* Washington was like. But I can tell you about the General. He was the most prim and proper a gentleman you could imagine. Some officers I've knowed could be quite human. But the General was by the book and expected the troops to be the same way. High and mighty ain't the word for it. And he might have been all for equality, but it was the kind that looks up and says, 'I'm as good as you,' and not the kind that looks down and says, 'You're as good as me.'"

He paused. The road was getting steeper and steeper, and Marybelle slower and slower. He gave her a slap of the leather, and she picked up the pace again.

"Mind you, we would have done any damn-fool thing he asked us, and we always did. There was a reason for it, if you figured it out. He didn't think he had to tell us. There was something supernatural about that man."

"He won us our freedom."

This time, the old man out and out cackled.

"That he did. But you know the best thing about the man? He could *lose* a battle. He lost battle after battle, but he still kept going, get us together, fight again, lose again, but kept on fighting. I figure he went on and on till the British was just tuckered out and give up. He got us our freedom by knowing better how to lose than the other fellow did till he finally won."

He patted the medallion again, fondly.

"That was the General."

As he paused, I heard a whispered discussion behind us

in the wagon, indistinct but urgent. Mr. Culpepper seemed oblivious to it, either too deaf to hear or too polite to notice. Perhaps he was just caught up in his memories.

"You should ask him yourself, Daisy," Mother raised her voice decisively. There was a shuffle of feet, and my sister suddenly popped her head over the wagon wall and poked it between us.

"Excuse me, mister. Could you stop for a minute? I have to use the necessary."

The old man had jumped a little when she'd appeared. Now he looked at her, squinting and frowning.

"The necessary? he asked.

"You know. The P-O-T," she whispered.

Mr. Culpepper immediately pulled the mare to a standstill. We creaked to a halt.

"You should have done that before we left," I said.

"I did," she said shortly. "I have to go again. Come help me down."

I sighed, raised my eyebrows, and climbed down. Daisy appeared over the piled bags and lowered herself over the side till I could grab her. It was hard to get a hold. Under the skirt of her gingham dress, her legs were jigging stiffly a mile a minute in an effort to hold it in. I set her down in the dust of the road, and she ran over and looked up expectantly at the old man, dancing in place. He looked back at her, bewildered.

"What?"

"Where's your chamber-pot?" Daisy was turning red, not with embarrassment, just effort.

Cumberland guffawed.

"About ten miles back that-a-way," he said. "Just go in the

bushes and squat."

"What?" Daisy's eyes were round. "In the wild? In the open?"

"Won't nobody look. Bob, you go with her a little way, make sure there's no varmints around. Not too far, mind."

She looked like she was struggling a little to get the concept straight in her head, but when I tried to take her hand, she wiggled it away and went haughtily ahead of me into the brush. Just five feet and we were under the eaves of the forest.

I looked around, picked up a stick, and beat the bushes. A few birds took off flapping, unseen in the canopy. I turned to Daisy.

"All right. Don't take too long, and don't get your shoes wet. Remember which way we came."

"Go along," she said fiercely, stamping the forest mold. I retreated back to the edge of the road.

It didn't take but a moment or two before she was strolling back, smiling and much more at ease.

"That wasn't so hard," she beamed as we went back to the wagon.

"Good lass," said Culpepper as I helped her scramble back up into the wagon. "You'll be a real mountain girl yet." I took my own seat again, and he set the mare in motion with a click of his tongue. For a while, I could hear Daisy excitedly describing her new experience to Mother until she finally settled into the pace of our progress.

I thought again about what the old man had been telling me.

"So, did George Washington ever…talk to you?"

He considered a moment.

"Not personally. But a friend of mine named Archer said

he overheard a conversation he had with one of his lieutenants that was mighty strange."

"Strange?"

"The General had just come back from the woods where he was praying. He did that, you see, away from the camp. Don't think he wanted to be seen begging, even from the Almighty. Anyways, he came back and told the lieutenant he'd met an uncanny creature in the woods."

I looked around at the forest we were threading through ourselves. The darkness under the trees seemed suddenly darker.

"A creature."

He turned to me, solemn as an owl.

"A deer. A snow-white deer that spoke in a lady's voice."

I swallowed. Back in the city I might have laughed. Out here, it seemed all too possible.

"What did it say?"

"All's Archer knows about it was that it had prophesied something about Washington. The General started to tell it, but noticed my friend listening where he was guarding the door. He closed it, so Archer never heard what the white doe had foretold. But the story went around, and we all got to figuring the General had a special destiny. First, we thought it was when Cornwallis surrendered, and later when he got to be president."

I let the tale sink in. Like I say, in the city, you're in a box. You can see the edges of everything, and when you turn the corner, you know the sort of thing you'll meet. Out here, I suddenly realized, there were no walls. Everything melted away before you and closed up behind you, and there was little or nothing but the road to tell you that humans had come this way. Who knew what strange thing you could meet until you suddenly met it?

We took another angling turn up the road and, suddenly, we met it. I drew in my breath sharply. So sharply that I was suddenly shadowed by the head of Mother raising herself up to look at what had surprised me so. I cast a fearful glance at her and saw Daisy pop her head up, too. By her stance I could tell she was standing tiptoe on the trunk.

There, by the side of the road, basking on top of a boulder overspread by a blanket, was an Indian—the first Indian I had ever seen. He was tall, and broad, and copper-colored, with two feathers drooping from his pewter hair. His shirt and fringed buckskin coat were draped drying on the rock next to him, and he was quite obviously deeply, seriously asleep.

Culpepper glanced at us and laughed.

"Don't you folks go worrying, now. That's just Old Thunder. Ain't no harm in him these days. He's always asleep." Culpepper spit over the side of the wagon. "He used to work for the Deacon on and off, but now that Whitley's passed away, Thunder just lays around snoozing, they say." He snorted. "Maybe when you get set up you can get him working again. But maybe not."

"Are there lots of Indians around here?" Daisy asked. "Pa says they're real good neighbors, if you get to know them."

"Not no more, missy. They all moved out and on. Thunder there's from one of the Five Nations. Never did hear which one."

We examined him closely as the wagon passed the man by. He had a beaky nose that rose like a prow from his broad face and twitched like he was sniffing something foul. Once he murmured some unknown word in a deep voice, but he never woke up as we trundled by.

"Your Pa's right about Indians," Culpepper said, long after Thunder was out of sight. "Treat them like men and they'll act like men. Treat them like dogs…well, they're going to bite. Just like anybody would. I've had white neighbors treated me worse than any one of the natives ever done."

We turned one last dog-leg in the road.

"Here's a fine example."

It was the house. The house we were obliged to take care of for a year if we were to have anywhere to live at all.

It was a mess.

It was small, smaller than any place I'd ever seen that wasn't just a shack and seemed smaller as it huddled right up against the mountain wall. It was maybe fifty feet long, and that was being generous.

True, the roof hadn't totally collapsed, but it was sway-backed, and the shakes were loose and slipping from their place. The chimneys at either end were grimy, the windows and door hung gaping and out of true, and patches of plaster had fallen from the walls to show the undressed stone underneath. The door handle and hinges drooled trails of rust.

The yard was overgrown with brush, but Mr. Culpepper took the wagon as close to the front door as it could go, then threw the reins down in disgust.

"Can't tell you how many times that crook Whitley cozened me. Cheated, threatened, bullied… Last thing he did was stick me with the accounts he'd run up afore I learned his true colors."

He spat again, then swung down out from the driver's seat.

"Well, come on. I might as well introduce you to your nearest neighbor."

He helped Ma and Daisy down from the back. My mother stood for a moment, looking at the house, assessing it like a general inspecting a battle line. Daisy clung to her skirt and was unusually quiet. But if Ma was daunted at all, she showed no sign of it.

"Well," she finally said. "We certainly have our task laid out for us." She turned to Mr. Culpepper. "Perhaps this neighbor you mention could be of some assistance to us, if we should require it."

The old man winced. His grin was more like a grimace.

"Oh, I don't think he'd be up to it, even if he were inclined to help. Come on. He ain't far."

He picked out a faint path to the left and headed into the thicket. The ferns were deep under the oak chestnuts and brushed the skirts of the womenfolk and the hem of Culpepper's coat. We didn't have far to go, though, only about five yards, when he stopped.

"This is it. This is his place."

It was a most peculiar thing. In the midst of a clearing was something like a stone hut, wider at the base than at the top. It stood on two concentric squares or steps of stone, the whole resting on a round base of dressed and mortared rock. The undergrowth stopped all around it, and not even a fallen leaf lay in that barren zone. After the slipshod house, it was almost shockingly pristine.

"Go on up and greet him, Bob. Though I don't think he'll answer back."

I hesitated, then started up the steps. As I got closer, I saw that what I had thought was another square stone in the building was a little window of transparent horn set in the rock, a trifle hazy but translucent. I looked back at the folks waiting below. I could tell Mother was expecting me to make a good impression, while Mr. Culpepper was just waiting to see what I would do.

I got to the top stair and stopped. I couldn't find any door or doorpost to knock. I raised my fist to tap on the window, standing on tiptoe and bringing my face close to the cloudy pane to peer inside. As the shadow of my head blocked the sunlight from glittering on the surface of the horn, I got a clear look at what was inside.

It was a dead man, scowling out at me.

"Holy hell!" I shrieked, stumbling back, nearly falling down the steps, but not before getting an all too clear look at the apparition inside.

He stood upright within, a tall thin man dressed in black, his withered hands crossed on his chest, clutching a moldering black book under crooked fingers. His eyes, though sunken, were shut, thank goodness. His nose had collapsed, and his lips drew back in a snarl that showed yellowed teeth. His balding forehead bulged in front like a pale discolored mushroom. In macabre contrast, his hair behind fell around his shoulders in thick, coiling chestnut curls.

"Bellamys," said Mr. Culpepper. "Meet Mr. Jerimoth Whitley. That evil old son-of-Satan."

"Mr. Culpepper, that was not a nice prank to pull on poor Robert at all." Mother had immediately shielded Daisy's eyes and drawn her in, throwing a sheltering arm around my shoulders as I ran to her side. Her voice was shaking once more in anger. "Not at all."

"I ask your pardon, Ma'am, but I had to show you," the old man said. He thumped his cane on the ground. "You need to see what you're up against. Once a body is buried, it can't be moved without extraordinary permission, you know that? Deacon Whitley had himself entombed up here in the woods and not down in the holy ground of the churchyard so he would never leave his land.

"People have started to call the mountain Deacon's Peak, and no one likes to come near this ill-omened place. It's cursed, it is, and no fit home for any living soul, much less a lady and her children alone."

"Nevertheless, I propose to make a home here." She pushed us forward, propelling us along the path back to the house. Culpepper reluctantly followed in her wake. "And there is much to do before dark, so if you will please help us unload our things before the light fails, I would be much obliged. As for dead men… Well, I believe they are considerably less dangerous than the living kind."

"It ain't fitting, and it's far too dangerous—" he began as we came out of the woods, then, "Hist, now!" he said, motioning us to silence.

There was movement on the far side of the yard. We watched tensely for a moment as the tall weeds shook, then relaxed as a pod of wild turkey started slowly and solemnly strutting out of the trees.

"Fine flock of birds," Culpepper said in hushed tones. "Look at that turkey cock. What a grand seigneur! If I only had my long rifle…"

There was the *crack* of a shot. The old man jumped, swearing. The flock took to the trees in flight, and the enormous bird he had been admiring fell to the earth, dead.

He turned to my mother in shock. She stood there calmly, a smoking pistol in hand. She walked across the yard in silence to her prize, and he followed dumbly in her wake. She lifted the calico-colored bird by its feet. Her shot had gone clean through its head, killing it instantly. He gazed at in in wonder.

"Dear lady," he finally croaked. "Such a shot…with such a gun…at such a distance. It ain't possible!"

"I have had some training," she said, wrapping the still-warm pistol up before tucking it away again in the bow at the back of her dress. "As you can see, I am not completely helpless. Shall we begin unloading?"

She added as an afterthought. "Would you care to come to supper this Sunday, Mr. Culpepper? We will be having roast turkey."

He bowed to her, hat in hand.

Chapter Three:
A Rocky Start

If I thought I was going to just turn over a pile of leaves and find the Deacon's secret gold, I was sadly mistaken.

Once we had half-leaned, half-kicked the door open, the inside of the cabin seemed a bizarre mixture of untouched by human hand and neglected. Rafters and corners were thickly covered in cobwebs, dust lay on every surface, even leaves clumped in shriveled, wind-blown piles on the floor. But the little place was far from empty.

We had expected, having discussed it on the trip from New York, that (apart from large articles of furniture) the house would probably be stripped bare. Hanging on the walls, lining the mantle-piece, peering from the shadows of a rough cabinet, were candlesticks, blackened pewter mugs, crockery, even a complete set of fire irons.

"I applaud the virtue of the people of Cumberton," Mother said. "After living in the city, I must say I half-expected to find the cabin cleared to the walls."

"Nobody cared to remove anything," Mr. Culpepper wheezed in the stirring dust. "Where do you want me to set your baggage?"

There wasn't much to choose from, as there were only two rooms. The larger room, the hall, was where we were standing. It was workroom, kitchen, and storeroom, all in one. A wall divided it off from the smaller room, the parlor. I poked my head in the door. It had a fireplace, too, and a writing table, and a bed at one end. One small window let hazy light through a horn shade. Mother looked in behind me.

"I believe the roof looks more stable here. If you will allow us a few moments of sweeping out, I think this place will serve for the night. We shall put everything in this room, then move our supplies to the proper place when all things are in order."

She looked down at Daisy and me.

"Children. Broom and dust cloths."

Mr. Culpepper took the chance to light up a pipe as we bustled for forty minutes of so. Ma took out a kerchief and tied her hair down. She dragged out the bedding, which was merely a shapeless sack filled with corn shucks, and set it against an outside wall to air. The moldy blanket that had been covering it, she tossed into the hall fireplace to be burned later. Then she took on old twiggy broom from the corner and began to attack in earnest, first the webs in the rafters, and then the dust on the floor.

Daisy, meanwhile, was laying siege to the furniture, adding its tribute of dust to floor, armed with a cloth that grew ever dingier at the battle progressed. After the first rank had fallen before her, she was ready to press her inroads even farther.

"Mama, where can I get some water? I need to wring out my rag."

"I'm sure I don't know, dear." She sneezed as she looked down, loose webs settling all around her. "Take Robert and ask Mr. Culpepper if he knows, and if he doesn't, scout around. But not too far."

I pulled my head out from where I had been looking up the parlor chimney. I had scrounged the old blanket as a makeshift sack, managed to clear the hearth of ash, and was examining the flue. Something had made a large, untidy nest up there, and I was trying to figure what I'd have to do to clear it. I was ready for a break.

"Come on, Daisy. Let's take a bucket. We can always use water."

"There's one in the hall." said Mother. "You can clean it out while you're there."

"Yes, Mama."

Outside, the old man was finishing his pipe and watching the shadows lengthen over the hills. He knocked out the bowl as we approached him.

"Mr. Culpepper, do you know where the well is?"

"'Tain't no well, but there's something just as good, and maybe better. Come on this a way."

He led us to the right, thankfully away from the gruesome monument on the left-hand path. I sighed inwardly with relief. The thought of having to pass that morbidity every time I wanted to get water had momentarily chilled me. As it was, we trudged about thirty yards around the hill before we came on a stream, purling quietly down from the heights.

"There you go," he said, pointing to a flat rock along the

bank. "You have to kneel, but there's no cranking up a bucket. Don't let the current take your pail off! It's a lot faster than it looks."

"Let me go first," I told Daisy.

I was glad I had been warned because the first tug of the stream almost pulled the handle out of my grip. Tightening my hold, I rinsed the dust and muck out as well as I could with bare hands. The current whirled it away downstream, and when I stood up, the water looked as clean as it did before.

"It's cold," I said.

"Melt from the mountains, boy. Come winter, it'll be even colder. But you won't find any clearer."

Daisy was next. She seemed fascinated with the billows of dirty water being carried away.

"It's like clouds in the sky," she said. "For fish."

"All right, it's clean enough," I said. "We got to get back to work. It'll be dark soon, and Mr. Culpepper has to get home."

"I'm comin'. Don't be such a fusspot, Bobbie."

We trooped back to the house, the full bucket banging at my knee and leaving a trail of sloshed water behind. I managed to get most of it back, though.

Inside, Ma had been very busy. The parlor looked almost livable. She had pinned the old blanket over the fireplace and, now, she had an immediate job for me.

She handed me the poker.

"Shinny on up there and knock down that nest, Robert. I want us to have a fire going as soon as night falls. It doesn't look too sooty, and you should be able to grip onto the stones fairly well. But please, be careful."

"Yes, Mama."

As I crawled behind the makeshift curtain, I saw Daisy

getting back to her dusting and Ma starting to direct the unloading and stowing of our luggage and supplies. I reached out, grabbed the poker, stuck it through my belt, then started my ascent.

I found the flue surprisingly clean. Not spotless, you understand, but not the caked-on black build-up I expected. I guess the wind and weather since the Deacon's passing might have taken care of some of that. But there was, here and there, white slimy drippings from the nest above. I did my best to avoid those.

There were plenty of rough handholds where the rocks inside protruded through the rough mortar. I found these were a blessing and a curse, as every now and then, I had to rest my fingers. I could do this by bracing my legs on one side of the flue and my back on the other. These rest periods were limited, however, by how long I could take the rocks' edges poking into my shoulders. Soon, I would be scrambling up again, poker clanking like a metal tail at my side, growing nearer and nearer to the tangled confusion ahead in the dim glow above.

I stopped just underneath the nest. I don't know what kind of bird had built it; something big and black, to judge by the feathers sticking out from the woven twigs. I pulled the poker out of my belt.

At first, I tried to just push it up and out, so I wouldn't have to worry about cleaning up after it. But it was jammed in so tight that it barely budged as I stuck the hooked iron end into it. Instead, the poker burst right through, sending a cascade of dust and bark right into my eyes and open mouth.

I sputtered and spat, squeezing my eyes shut. Suddenly, I was disgustedly angry. This was war now. I yanked the poker out, head down, back and legs braced, and began to stab the offending bundle again and again, yelling I don't know what nonsense with each blow. I seem to remember shouting, "Yah! Yah!" and starting, then choking off curses, as wild blows rang off the chimney stones and sticks, filth and old egg shells cascaded into my lap and down to the hearth below.

When I finally saw clear again, the sky above me was a deep blue, and the light was long and golden. With my left hand still clutching my weapon, I brushed debris out of my hair and off my clothes. The top was so temptingly near, the air above so clean after the clouds of conflict, I knew I had to go on up, look out, and breathe the freedom I had won. I started the last scrabble up.

The space that I spread my elbows out into was intoxicating after the cramped prison of the flue. My head swam for a minute, and I closed my eyes, clutching grimly to the brim of the well of stones that yawned below me. It couldn't be more than twenty feet, but to my feelings, it might as well have been a hundred. When my head settled down, and my breathing was back to normal, I opened my eyes.

The valley was spread out below me, like a dark green blanket. It was trees, all trees. Some darker, some lighter, but standing so close that the wind rippling over them seemed like a field of wheat. The road was invisible. The town was invisible, far down the slope. Only a thin thread of smoke suggested where it might be. To the left and the right, the hills rose higher and higher towards me until they seemed to break like waves on the high point where we stood. The shadows of clouds passed over them like ships. I turned to look behind me and almost flinched.

The mountain was frowning down on me. It looked like

that huge mass was ready to topple over on us. Seen from below, it had seemed solid, almost sheltering. Somehow, from my perch, it appeared impossible that it would stay established, that anything that big could hang there and not crumble, collapse, and cover us at the slightest whim.

I shuddered. Even the wind that was starting to gather seemed to threaten the balance. I ducked, pulled my head in, and started my cautious way back down.

Down was worse than up, with gravity pulling at my shirt tails, ready to yank me to the stone below. When I finally reached the bottom, I stood a moment, arms shaking with effort, my feet scuttling in the garbage from the nest. I wasn't exactly scared, just sort of relieved. After the dust of my descent settled, I opened the curtain and stepped out.

"It's done," I said.

Ma turned, took one look at me and sent me out with a clean set of clothes to change in the hall. I looked around me as I left the parlor. I wouldn't say the room was spotless, but it was certainly human again, and filling up with our belongings. Daisy had finished her dusting and was sitting at the desk, legs kicking at the rungs of the chair, solemnly watching Mr. Culpepper unloading our supplies as Mother directed their disposal.

Once I had changed and rattled the dust out of my hair outside, I helped the bent old man with the last of our things. The trunk with all our good clothes and personal items was the last piece in. I helped place it at the foot of the still-empty bed frame.

"Well, it looks like you'll have this place right and fit in no time," Mr. Culpepper said, moving an appraising eye over our progress. He took off his hat and bowed again to Mother, and then bowed to Daisy and me, much to my sister's delight.

"I'll be off back to the trading post again. If you need anything—if you have any emergencies or alarms—don't hesitate to call on me."

"Thank you again, very much, sir." Ma actually curtsied, a full curtsy, as pretty as any I'd ever seen. The fact that she was covered in dust and her hair still bound in a kerchief only made it seem more graceful. "You have been of very great service to us."

"Glad to help such nice folks."

We all followed him outside to see him off. He pulled himself up into his cart with creaking effort and gathered the reins. He looked down at us one last time.

"Ya'll take care now. Get your fire lit and keep indoors after nightfall. All sorts of critters out after dark around here. And, you children, don't forget to say your prayers now. I'll see you on Sunday, Mrs. Bellamy, if not before!"

With a, "Huddup, girl!" he got the mare moving, and it wasn't long before the wagon had turned the corner and was out of sight. It suddenly seemed very quiet. We were all alone.

"Now then, my dears," Ma said, briskly breaking the silence, "If we're going to have something to sleep on, we'd better start gathering some bedding. The plant overgrowing our yard looks to be goose-grass, so we can clear our front porch and make our bed at the same time."

So, me armed with my pocketknife, and Ma with her kitchen shears, we began cutting down huge bundles of flowering, bouncy weeds. Behind us, Daisy bundled them up and carried them inside to start a pile on the ropes of the bed-frame. We only stopped when the sun touched the rim of the purpling hills and the approaching shadows of the forest chilled the clearing.

"That will have to do," Ma announced. "We need to get the fire going before we lose the light."

"Couldn't we light a lantern?" Daisy asked.

"We could, but that would use up oil. Let's save that while we still have good daylight."

We trooped in, past the still-desolate hall and into the parlor, which looked even more crowded with the pile of goose-grass towering in the bed corner. That was soon crushed down into a more accessible size when Ma took out a feather quilt from the chest, and with Daisy's help, spread it over the pile. Meanwhile, I laid down the kindling for the fire.

There were piles of logs next to the fireplace, almost to the roof. When I pulled some of them off to lay on top of the trash from the old nest and drifted leaves that I had gathered, I heard something alive *crickling* around over the bark. My mind ran over everything from spiders to lizards to rats, and simply hoped that our presence would be enough to drive them off in time. There was nothing to do now but build the fire.

Our tinderbox was in good condition, and the wood dry and seasoned, but even so, it took me several tries to get it going. The last light of day was rapidly going from the small high window when it finally was burning bright and clear, throwing warm shadows over the little parlor, which suddenly looked cozy and secure.

"Well done, Robert," said Ma. "Let's shut up for the night."

We closed the cabin door and barred it from within. For an extra precaution, we knocked some wood wedges in under it and laid a couple of logs wherever we could still see light coming through. Then we withdrew into the parlor, and as a barrier to the yawning darkness of the hall, pinned a blanket over the doorway between.

"Now, let's have some dinner, and then to bed. I think we've done very well for our first day."

We finished off the last of our travel rations: half a loaf of staling bread, some squashy cheese, a few apples, and a canteen of lemonade.

When we finished, we sat a bit, looking into the shifting embers of the fire. Daisy yawned, and cuddled a little closer to mother.

"What are we goin' to do tomorrow?"

"Well, I shall have to try my hand at cooking, first thing. It's been a while, but I suppose biscuits are still biscuits. We shall need to get some chickens, some time or other, if we want really nice breakfasts."

"Then what?"

"More cleaning, repair, and wood, I should think. We shall need a lot of wood to get through the winter."

Daisy looked drowsily around the room.

"We got wood."

"Not near enough."

Daisy sighed.

"Will we ever get to play again?"

"There'll be plenty of time for play, and talking, and reading, when we've got long evenings when it'll be too cold for anything else. Then you'll be glad we got ready. Anyway, right now, it's time for bed."

I just kept my nose stuck in the corner while they changed into their night gowns. When I turned around again, they were standing next to the bed. Ma was showing Daisy where the necessary was for the night.

"Your turn to get ready, Bob."

I raked to fire together and banked the embers. Ma and Daisy climbed on top of the quilt. The bedstraw grass crumbled farther down in a complaining hiss. In the embers glow, I took off my shoes and leggings and put them next to the bed, then climbed in. The bed crumpled down even more, but there was still some good spring in it, so you could tell you weren't just lying on ropes and rocks.

"Let's say our prayers, darlings."

Mother led the way, thanking the Lord for all the things we had and the good things that had happened. She did it in that voice formally addressing God, but pitched also, I think, to encourage us kids about the situation we were in. I added a few riders about blessing Mr. Culpepper and his help, and about watching over us through the night. Daisy rounded things out by asking Him to take care of Pa, wherever he was and whatever he was doing, and send him back soon. That struck us all solemn, and after a meek, "Amen," we all settled back to sleep.

But I couldn't. Maybe it was the firelight in my eyes, maybe it was plain worry. I listened as first Daisy's breath got slow and regular, and I knew she was asleep, then Mother relaxing and murmuring as she drifted off. After a while, I heard the skittering in the woodpile, and the *pop* of the embers as they burned up and fell in on themselves, and then the moaning of the wind as it began to pick up and cut around the corners of the house. Whenever I shifted, trying to settle down, the bedding shushed me.

The one thing that was really bothering me, I found, was that one window. I kept looking up at it. It was too high to worry about critters, and almost certainly too small to worry about people. I kept looking at it like it was watching me. There was something creepy about it I couldn't figure out, till it suddenly flashed on me. It was covered in horn, just like the little window in the Deacon's grave.

With that realization, my memory immediately brought up that decaying face before my eyes, forgotten in the busyness of work, and seemed to print it right on that window. My imagination began to picture those withered eyelids slowly opening, those wrinkled lips drawing back in a grin, baring— yes, of course! —blunt yellow teeth like broken tombstones, and looking at me. Straight at me.

The spell was broken by a sudden, soundless flash of lightning that wiped the window clean as a slate. I jumped, then jumped again as seconds later, a low *brool* of thunder shook to house to its bones. The wind followed it, howling, angry.

The second peal was much closer and woke Ma and Daisy up.

"What is it?" Daisy squealed. "Is the mountain coming down?"

Ma drew her close.

"Hush, child, it's just a storm. You've been through storms before." She reached out and clutched me tight, too. I was glad when she did that, but it didn't take away the fear of the next crash, which lit the night with purple lightning and doused the fire with a sudden deluge of rain.

The room went black. Steam billowed in, illuminated by the flashes for a second at a time into solid curling sculpture, pierced by the needles of water that started streaming from the roof. The rain pounded down like a fist battering at the shingles. Everything was a chaos of noise and light and movement. For what seemed forever, we sat up huddled together on the bed, hoping each blast of lighting was the last, jumping with each new explosion, followed by Ma's breathless speech, trying to comfort us, but coming too quick to soothe.

At last, miraculously, the thunder moved away until it was only a grumble, and then went quiet. The wind stopped howling, then grieved for a while, then was still. At last the drizzle of the rain was the loudest sound, dripping in and spattering in the darkness with a voice like desolation.

We sat up, eyes puckering into the dark. Luckily (or perhaps by design), the roof over the bed had been the most sheltered bit of all.

"What should we do?" asked Daisy.

"What is there to do?" said Mother. "Let's try to get some sleep and see how things look in the morning."

We settled back in. Tired out by fear, exhausted with travel and work, despite the chill and dark and damp, we went to sleep at last.

I woke up early the next morning, when the first light touched the house. I got dressed, unpinned the cloth from the doorway, knocked away the wedges from the front door, kicked it open, and grabbed the old broom. Before Ma and Daisy had even got up, I had swept the standing water on the floor out of the parlor, into the hall, and out the doorway. Mother woke to the clanking as I used a shovel to clean the sludge out of the fireplace.

"Good morning," I said. "It's a beautiful day."

It was. Outside, the air was scrubbed, the sun was just rising into clear blue sky free of any cloud. Long gold bars of light were turning the morning mist into a glory under the trees. Inside, the rays were starting to chase shadows out of their corners.

"Good morning, Robert. It's nice to see you already busy."

"I should have the fire going again soon."

"Very good. Then I'll make some breakfast."

She rose up and changed into some work clothes as I labored over the fire, choosing the driest wood I could find and hustling up more kindling. I remembered there were some wood-shavings in the packing. They were still dry and just the thing to catch the spark. The fire was going well, and I was feeling drier than I had in hours, when Ma came up to me with the chamber pot.

"Go empty this, please."

"Where?"

"Just somewhere far from the house and the drinking water. We'll figure out a regular spot later."

I paused in the yard. Not near the water, so not to the right. That meant to the left, in what I was already calling Whitley's Woods.

I braced myself. The morning sun helped. I thought about walking right on up the steps and sloshing it on that old corpse's stones, in defiance. Well, under the trees that way, anyway. I thought that we wouldn't be heading out that way much.

I was just about to enter the woods when I suddenly heard "Wait!" and Daisy came running up, still in her night dress. She pulled up next to me.

"Gimmie that!" she yelped, grabbing the necessary out of my hand and fleeing into the undergrowth. She emerged a moment later.

"Okay, go on."

I sighed, went a few yards in. I could just see the stones among the trees when I decided that was far enough, my bravado evaporating under the solemn stillness. I hustled back out.

Daisy was waiting for me, and we walked back together. My stomach rumbled.

"I wonder what Ma is making." In the morning air, with the prospect of breakfast ahead, the day seemed full of promise.

"Let's find out."

Daisy skipped ahead, and I started trotting after. We reached to door together. We rushed into the parlor and stopped short.

Mother was sitting, absolutely still, next to the fifty-pound bag that was our entire ration of flour. It was open, and we could see that rather than fine powder, it was full of mushy paste. A thin white liquid seeped from it onto the floor.

"Ruined," she said.

Chapter Four:
A Stone's Throw

We stood stock-still, as the fact and its consequences sank in. Money wasted, cooking supplies destroyed, breakfast gone. Daisy's face went beet red.

"What do we do now?" she wailed. She punched the flour bag. It squelched and oozed more muck onto the dirt floor of the hall. This made her even more angry, and she kicked it as if the sack had got wet on purpose.

"Maybe this place is cursed," I muttered.

I looked up at the roof. Golden morning sun gleamed, mocking, through latticed holes. If only it hadn't rained. If only it had held off for one more day. I felt that some sort of doom, an evil fate, had been chasing us since Father disappeared and had caught up with us, maybe even lured us out here to pounce on us in the wilderness.

"Well, what *do* we do now?" I asked.

Mother raised her head as if it were a cannon, slow and heavy but inexorable. She aimed it at the world.

"I think," she said, "that we will have oatmeal for breakfast instead."

I looked at her in disbelief, and then, almost awe. Flour was vital to so much of our survival, such a huge element in our cookery, and such a big chunk of our expenses, that its loss was enough to sink us before we had really started. I know I felt ready to march to the nearest poorhouse, or worse, go crawling to Gramma Morrison to ask for her cold, triumphant, long-prophesied charity. But Ma wasn't licked yet. She handed me a cook-pot.

"Go fetch some water, Robert."

I raced out through the damp grass to the stream and was back in a trice. I hung the pot over the fire, and as the ice-cold water began to heat, Ma set us around the little table to have a council of war.

"Is there any way we can use the flour?" Daisy began. "Can we dry it out, or cook some of it at least, or somethin'?"

"I'm afraid not. The water's been sieved through the roof, and there's all sorts of foulness mixed in with it. Long before it's dry it will be moldy. I don't know. There may be some use for it, but none that I'm aware of. That's one of the reasons I fear I shall have to go back to Cumberton."

"On foot?" I exclaimed.

She smiled.

"It's the only way. And needs must, you know."

She glanced over at the fire and stood up. She took a couple of handfuls of oats from their small barrel and threw them into the seething water and began stirring them.

"I shall start right away after breakfast. With any luck, I may be able to get a ride back up the hill and be back before nightfall."

"What about Daisy and me?"

"You must stay here," she said firmly. "I shall go faster if I'm by myself, and I'm not sure Daisy could take the trip."

"Hey!"

"Come on, you know I'd end up carrying you," I said. "You couldn't make it even ten blocks, back in town."

She frowned but didn't argue.

"Well, what are we supposed to do until you get back?"

"Do whatever comes to your hands to do. Clean up. Gather wood. Cut more weeds. You could read to your sister and do some studying. But most of all, look around and think about everything you see. Think about what could happen, and what you would do, and how best to do it. I'll be back before you know it, and you can report to me all that you've figured out."

By this time, the mush was bubbling thickly. Ma pulled it off the fire and added some shavings off the sugarloaf and a pat of salted butter from the supplies. When it had all melted into a wonderful sticky mess, it was doled out in three bowls, and ten minutes was spent in silence broken only by the accidental scraping of spoons. Finally, Mother pushed her bowl away with a precise gesture.

"Your first chore, Bob, will be to find me a sturdy stick, suitable for walking. I will be getting ready. Daisy, prepare the dishes for scrubbing."

"Yes'm."

I took the hatchet and went out, headed for a stand of saplings I had noticed before. It wasn't long before I found a good one, about as thick as a man's thumb, and had hacked it down, stripped it, and cut it to size. When I brought it into the hall, Mother had banked the fire and was dressed in her traveling gaberdine, pinning her hat on.

"Thank you, Bob." She accepted the stick. "That is just right."

"Don't forget the trail down. Did you hear Mr. Culpepper say there's a straight foot trail that cuts right to town? If you strike it, you can save some time, if you think you're up for it."

"I shall certainly look out for it."

She pounded the walking stick twice on the floor, as if to test it, set it against the doorjamb, then straightened and addressed us formally.

"Now, at any sign of danger, get in and bar the door. I have hidden your Father's rifle there in the woodpile. Bob, you are not to touch it except in direst need and, Daisy, not at all, do you understand? Very good."

I stood straight and tried to look manly. I had shot it once or twice when Pa was around, without much success as to accuracy, but I thought I could handle it. Daisy looked jealous of my responsibility. I think Ma noticed and adjusted her plan accordingly.

"Now, Daisy, I have a special task for you."

She walked over to the cupboard and took down the bee-hive barrel. She set it on the table, unscrewed the lid, then walked over and reached into the bed. She pulled out a bundle wrapped tightly in a handkerchief. It clinked slightly.

"This," she said sternly, "Is all the money we have left in the world. If we must, we will have to pay Mr. Culpepper from this."

She put in in the jar with a dull clunk and turned the lid tight.

"I'd rather not carry it with me, so I'm leaving it here." Back into the shadows of the shelf it went. "Daisy, you are in special charge of the money, since it's your barrel."

Daisy beamed, and tried to stand so straight she was on her tiptoes. I had a hard time keeping a serious face.

"Yes, ma'am," she said. "I'm on the guard. Nothin' will mess with it while I'm around!"

She looked around.

"Bobbie, get me a stick, too. I need somethin' to whack with!"

Ma smiled.

"Heart of a lion, my child!"

She moved to the door and took up her stick.

"And now, I simply must get a move on. Remember all I have told you, be careful, and wish me luck!"

She bent down and kissed and hugged us both, and we all walked out, her arms still around us, until she reached the road. We parted and she headed down the trail. Daisy and I watched till she reached the curve. She turned, we all waved again to each other, and then with a furl of her cloak, she was gone from our sight.

"All right," I said. "Let's wash up."

"No. I said I want a stick."

I groaned.

"Very well, I'll get you one. If a bear comes up on us while we're cleaning the dishes, you can hit it on the nose."

She squinted up at me.

"Are you tryin' to be funny?"

I sighed.

"I'll just get you a stick. Come on. There's a good place for some out by the stream. We'll take the crockery with us."

We licked every bowl clean first (no sense wasting a taste), and the pot, too, before lugging them to the water side. We scrubbed them out using sand and laid them to dry on a rock in the sun while I chopped down a stick for Daisy. Just her size, and slender, too, and a little whippy. She switched it back and forth as we headed back to the cabin. I carried the crockery.

"Yip! Yah! Take that, you blackguard!" she yelled, snicking the heads off of any weed daring to raise its head higher than its fellows.

"Save some of your strength for the house," I said. "I'm sure there are plenty of little beasties there that can use a pummeling."

"The house," she said. "It's more like a chicken coop than a house."

She took another swish at a nodding stalk of goldenrod. "I hate it."

"It's not so bad. It just needs a little care, is all."

We came up and started for the front door.

"I don't think it had much love from Mr. Whitley." I shuddered, and looked off left to the darkling woods. The sun didn't seem to penetrate there so much as the right-hand way.

"I don't think I'd like it much more if I thought it had," said Daisy. "I'd like to spit in that ugly old scarecrow's eye."

We went in.

"Anyway, we're here now," I said. "Let's fix it up good and show Deacon Whitley who's in charge of the place."

"Yeah!"

We went to work with a will. First, I swept the rain and flour mush out the door. Somehow, between us, Daisy and I heaved the oozing sack out of the parlor and into the hall and applied ourselves to that front room. Although it was larger, it was much barer, and so simpler to clean. Even the fireplace in it, enormous as it was, seemed cleaner, as if much unused, and perhaps because of its size was free of any clogging nest. By noon, we stopped, staring around. There didn't seem to be much else we could do.

"What do we do now?" asked Daisy.

"How about lunch?"

This proved to be a bit of a poser. There wasn't much of anything, uncooked, we could dine on. Eventually, we settled on a strip of jerked beef and a dried applejohn each. When we finished, our stomachs were still rumbling, but we didn't dare try anything more complicated.

"I want more meat," said Daisy.

"No."

"Why not?"

"Because I'm not having Ma come home to find we've eaten everything up, that's why."

"But I'm hungry."

I looked around and tried to think, like Ma had said. I started to go over what we had packed away, trying to think of something to do to divert Daisy and get her mind off food when, suddenly, an idea struck me.

"Just a minute."

I went over to my pack and started to dig through my sparse belongings. I reached past my clothes, a cloth pouch of marbles, my good shoes, and came up triumphantly.

"A-ha," I beamed, holding up my prize.

Daisy looked at it skeptically.

"Your sling? What are you going to do, make soup out of it?"

I suppose my sling, and what such a thing is, needs a bit of description these days. It's pretty simple: a leather cradle sits in the middle of it, with two long cords on either side. One cord has a loop at the end to hold it on your finger. The other has a knot on the end. You put a stone or a marble or a bit of lead in the cradle, hold both ends, get the sling whirling, pick a target, and let the knot end go at just the right minute.

It sounds crazy, but once it gets whirling, it hits with surprising force and accuracy. I have to say I prided myself on my aim and my instrument and was a little hurt by my sister's remark.

"I'm taking it out to get you something to eat. There's bound to be something edible running around in these woods. I'm going foraging."

That made her pause. Her face twisted.

"Do...do you really think you should?"

"Yes, I do. When Ma gets back, by golly, things will be better than when she left."

"Can I go with you?"

I was excited, on fire with sudden inspiration. I wasn't really listening to her.

"No, you got to stay here."

"Please?"

"No, you have to watch the house." I really didn't want her tagging along. I felt this was my adventure, and I thought it was better I went alone. I had to put her off.

"And the money," I added. "That's your job you know. Ma told you."

That shrank her back a bit. She'd never consider going against a duty Ma set her. She looked a little wild-eyed.

"What about what she told you?"

"'Whatever your hand finds to do, do it,'" I repeated.

"Well, don't go far."

"I won't."

"And don't get lost!"

"I won't."

"And start back before dark!"

"I will. Dang it, Daisy, don't worry!"

I checked my pocket knife.

"I'll be back before you know it. Why don't you try reading something while I'm out? Spell your way a little through some Shakespeare."

She snorted.

"Even when I can read the words, I can't hardly get any sense out of `em."

"Keep at it, and one day you'll be as clever as your big brother." I took my cap from the peg near the door.

"Now, I'm off."

I bowed.

"Goodbye, goodbye. Parting is such sweet sorrow, so I shall say goodbye till it be morrow."

"You better come back before tomorrow, or you'll find a snake in your bed one day soon!"

I laughed.

"It's your bed too!"

"Yes, but I'll know it's there, and you won't know when it's comin'!"

I laughed and left. The last thing I saw going out the door was her red face, furious, and I realize now, furiously anxious.

Once outside, I was faced, again, with that choice. The dark woods past the grave to the left or the already more familiar way by the stream to the right. I was able to salve any feelings of uneasiness by the logical decision that I could get some good water-smoothed stones for the sling if I went right.

After selecting about seven or eight good ones, and balancing them between my pockets, I found a shallow place across the chilly water, took off my shoes, and made my way to the other side. As I sat on a boulder, putting my shoes back on, I looked into the unknown before me and considered.

There are probably a few places today like the woods I was facing, but not many, and not a whole lot of people see them. Huge trees, gnarled, old, which had been growing for centuries, interlaced their arms until all was perpetual twilight underneath. In that gloom, very little grew, and it was like walking in an empty hall carpeted with the fallen leaves of a hundred years.

I figured I might have two hours at best to scout around, if I were to head back with any light to find my way. I took out my sling, loaded a stone, and entered the trees like a burglar making his way into a sleeping mansion.

Luckily, I wasn't completely green, or I would have been lost after the first half hour. But Pa had taken me out scouting since I was two years old, so I knew a thing or two.

The most important thing to do is to leave yourself a trail, little marks to help find your way back home. Nicks in trunks of trees, sticks pointing the way you came, piles of stones, if you can find them. Every ten paces or so, I halted and scrupulously set a sign and scanned the trees.

About an hour in, my vigilance was rewarded. I had stopped and was considering my next mark when movement ahead caught my eye. There, in a little clearing made by its own downfall, was the bole of an enormous chestnut oak, and scampering over it, in and out a hole, was a fat gray squirrel.

Now the only difference between a squirrel and a rat is diet and a fluffy tail, but a nut-fed squirrel, cooked right, can be a fine sweet piece of meat. I calculated the distance and thought my chance of a hit was good. I didn't dare try to get any closer. The rattle of leaves and snap of twigs would surely alert my prey, no matter which way the wind was blowing. I got my sling whirling, slow at first, then it was a blur, and at the fatal point of velocity, let loose.

With a sharp *crack* it hit, three inches from the foot of the squirrel, right on the tip of the entrance of its lair. He was gone in an instant, sprinting away from the toppled trunk. I swore—a rather sharp word, since I was alone. It was answered by a loud *creak*.

I listened, mystified, as the fallen tree seemed to groan in pain. There was a sudden *snap*, a sodden explosion, and then the mixed horde of the squirrel's nuts came spilling out like an avalanche from the wasted wood.

I went running over eagerly. The little beast was gone, and with it the chance of meat, but this was almost better. Nuts we could eat, either right from the shell or plainly roasted, without any real cookery. I knelt down by the spill and started scooping it together.

It was a rather motley lot, including some pretty inedible acorns, but it was mostly hickory, beech, and chestnuts. I pulled the hole open further and recovered even more than had fallen out. I made a bag out of my shirt and gathered them all up. Once they were secure, I thought it was time to head back. I stood up and looked around.

I had a moment of panic when I realized that in my eagerness over the squirrel, I hadn't set my last marker. But my shuffle through the leaves had left a faint trail, and I was able to find my way back to the track.

Though I had to cast my way around once or twice, I was able to make my way back by my signs fairly easily. When I finally found myself out of the woods and at the water's side again, I was feeling pretty pleased with myself. After I crossed the stream, I was happily humming, heavy-laden shirt full of food in my hands, thinking of the praise no doubt coming my way, when I heard Daisy screaming.

Chapter Five:
Unwelcome Party

I froze for an instant, as all kinds of thoughts whirled in my head. Of snakes. Of bears. Of broken arms. Of fire. What had I done, leaving my little sister all alone in the wilderness? Just a second ago, it had seemed like a fine idea. Now, I desperately wanted to call back time, like it was a china plate headed for the floor that could still be caught before it broke, even as I heard it shattering. Then I ran for the house, my bundle now in an iron grip, evidence, at least, of my good intentions.

As I turned the bend, I slammed to a halt. A tumult of angry voices filled the air, mingled with the whinny and stamp of horses, Daisy's voice screeching through it all.

There were obviously people in the house, quite a few people, and they sounded angry. And if people were the problem, it came to me I'd best approach with caution. I looked around desperately, wondering what I could do.

I looked at the cabin. The little window was too high to reach, but while I scanned it, my eyes went to the roof and the hill above it. If I could climb up the hillside, I saw, I could get on the roof and look down the holes.

No sooner thought of than begun. I spilled the nuts out of their temporary bag and put my wrinkled shirt back on to save my skin. Then I went quickly back along the wall of the hill until I found a likely place of ascent and began to scramble up. It was pretty steep, but with the help of vines and stubby saplings trying to grow into the rock, I was able to clamber to the grassy slope above. Then it was a vertical fight against gravity to crab-walk my way to the cabin, carefully lower myself to where the hill met the eaves of the house, and as quietly as possible get on the roof.

It groaned alarmingly as I put my weight on it, but the beams were sound, thank heaven, and the noise of the fight below must have drowned out the creaking as I knelt and put my eye to a crack. Either that, or they were just too busy to hear. Daisy was apparently putting up quite a fight.

The first thing I heard clear was her bawling.

"Put that down! Put that back! That doesn't belong to you!"

I followed her voice and focused on it through the mill of activity below. Men were churning through the little house, grabbing up our belongings, stuffing them in sacks, and running in and out. In the corner by the bed, a lady, in rather travel-worn finery, stood clenching Daisy out of the way, and having a hard time of it, dividing her attention between keeping an eye on the work and avoiding my sister's random but vicious kicks.

"MacCallister! MacCallister, hurry the men up! I can't hold

this little termagant much longer!"

"Let me have a crack at her, sir," one of the men said, grinning, his beady eyes squinting. He never paused at his work. "One little tap, and she won't give us trouble no more."

The man addressed bridled.

"Never let it be said," he declaimed, "That Captain MacCallister's men ever harmed a lady, even a screeching little sprat of a lady." He came down a little from his high horse. "Pay attention to your job, Grisly Joe, so we can get out of here."

Grisly Joe turned away, disappointed. I studied this MacCallister, obviously the man in charge. He stood a little apart from the other fellows, moving slow and stately around the bustle. His main goal seemed to be picking out choice items from the loot. I noticed with displeasure that he was clutching our Shakespeare, and the pocket watch Pa had given me was dangling carelessly in his gloved hands. His big cocked hat, dripping with lace, was possibly the fanciest I'd ever seen, on man or woman.

Now that my eye was adjusting, I observed that there were only five members to the gang. The smallness of the cabin and the rushing activity had magnified their impression. There was the Captain, the lady, Grisly Joe, and two others. Only five, but to me on my own, they were trouble enough.

"No, Billy, put that down."

One of the others, a scrawny old man, had started to load firewood into a gunny sack. The tall black man who had addressed him took the sack and wood gently away. The old man smiled back toothlessly and turned elsewhere for employment. The black man emptied the sack glockling to the floor and went back to hefting the larger barrels and boxes out to the waiting horses.

"Stupid old beggar," said Joe. He slammed a frying pan—our frying pan! —into his sack with a clang. "Worse than useless. Don't know why Daft Billy's still in the gang."

"He's a dab hand with the horses," said the lady. "He loves the beasts. Who would take care of them if he was gone? You, Joe?"

"No, ma'am, Mrs. MacCallister." He sulked, head lowered.

"They don't like you, do they, Joe?" the black man said cheerfully as he walked back in. "You 'member when Aunty Rosy bit you?"

Grisly Joe dropped his bag and squared off on him, fists clenched, legs dancing furiously beneath him. The big man must have been three times his size.

"Shut up, Sugar! Shut up, or so help me you'll be bust up!"

For all his size, Sugar seemed alarmed at the bantam jigging in front of him. It made me wonder what experience he must have of the man's rages.

"All right, all right. I'm sorry. Don't get riled now."

Grisly Joe backed off, no less angry it seemed, and went back to thrusting our rapidly disappearing movables into his loot bag, muttering sharply under his breath. Captain MacCallister, in the meanwhile, had sailed airily over the whole incident. He now descended momentarily out of his cloud.

"By the way, it's Rocinante, Sugar. Not Aunty Rosy. The horse's name is Rocinante. Please get it right for future reference."

Mrs. MacCallister gazed adoringly at her beau.

"Someday, it'll all be in the history books."

"That's right, Dolly m'dear." He kissed his free hand to her.

Suddenly, Daft Billy crowed. Everyone looked up, startled.

While they had been talking, he had randomly climbed up the shelves of the cabinet-with bare, dirty feet, I noticed, and was now holding out and triumphantly shaking his newly discovered prize.

It was the money jar.

"Oho, I detect the clink of cash," cried Mrs. MacCallister. "It looks like this will be a paying enterprise, for once!"

The old man jumped to the floor, rather nimbly for all his years, and walked forward vaguely.

"No!"

Daisy had quieted down to watch while the gang quarreled, so quiet that the lady had relaxed her grip somewhat and almost forgotten her. Now, she leaped away and snatched the little barrel from Billy's unresisting hands. The old man just smiled and wandered amiably off, but the rest of the gang surged in. The first one to try to take it away was the lady.

"Give it here!" she said grimly. "Give me that!"

Daisy curled herself around the jar with her whole body, head, legs, and arms, and just rolled away from Mrs. MacCallister's prying fingers. The lady stepped back, red and puffing. The Captain stepped in and tried to assert his authority.

"Little girl!" he huffed. His gloves couldn't seem to find any purchase on Daisy's tightly wound and frantically careening globe. "I order you to release that money, or face the dire consequences!"

"My Momma told me to guard it, and she's the one who gives me orders!"

MacCallister stood helplessly stymied, but Grisly Joe cut in.

"Give us the god-damn money, or so help me, lord, I'll break your little neck!"

He got a sharp little kick in the eye for that. He fell on his rear, howling and cursing. Daisy's leg was back in position before anyone could grab it.

"Don't swear," she said severely.

"Come on, honey, let it go," said Sugar, bending down and trying to pull the canister away. I thought for sure she'd have to let go under the pressure of his enormous strength, but then it became obvious after a minute that wasn't happening.

"Can't you even overpower a little girl?" snorted Mrs. MacCallister.

"I don't want to hurt the child," Sugar said sadly.

"Well, I do," said Joe, who had finally managed to get up, eyes watering. He grabbed a block of wood. "Let me try again."

"Enough!" blustered MacCallister, raising his hand. "We don't have time for this! The law might descend upon us at any minute. If the girl won't let go of the spoils, she'll just have to come with us. Sugar, load her up! We ride!"

My heart sank. I had thought that when they left, disastrous as the robbery was, it was not total as long as I could reunite with Daisy afterward. But if she were gone, how could I ever face our mother again?

The gang was swiftly packing up. Sugar had a bag of cornmeal under one arm, and Daisy under the other. MacCallister proceeded out with his relatively light load, and his missus following him, Ma's scanty supply of dresses over her arm. Dresses way too small, let me add, for her ample form. Grisly Joe took the time to snap the old broom in half and hurl his block of wood, cracking the horn window. I believe he would have set the place on fire if the embers hadn't gone out. He was the last to leave, spitting on the floor as he exited.

I raised my head cautiously and looked out front. I could

hear the jingling and creaking of harness and the stamping of impatient hooves, and then I saw them ride out, twelve horses altogether, some packed with all our belongings and others laden with the robbers, MacCallister at their head.

I stood up taller, craning after them as they thundered off. I could just see Daisy where she sat, curled up in front of Sugar. It looked like she was still squeezing the beehive jar close to her. I especially noted where they entered the woods to the west, next to a huge fir tree with a hanging broken branch turned brown. Then I shinnied my way down the roof, dropped to the ground, and hurried inside.

I had had just one hope, and it had both flared up and been almost instantly extinguished when the crazy old coot had started fiddling with the woodpile, then flared again when they stopped him. I ran over and began scrabbling the logs away until I uncovered my father's rifle.

I gingerly, almost reverently, pulled it from its hiding place. I knew it was loaded. I know this is dangerous, but it takes quite a while to prepare such a gun, and in emergencies, one seldom has the time. I took the bag of shot snugged away near the butt and slung the powder horn next to it over my shoulder. I thought of what Pa taught me, and what Ma had said, and judged that if there was any time to take it up, it was now.

I was moving like clockwork now. I went outside, picked up some sticks, and sighted where the fir with the broken branch was. I made an arrow on the ground, pointing the way, so anyone who found it would at least have some clue of the direction I was taking. I stood up, squared my shoulders, and lit out after them.

On the open ground, the grass from their passing was already springing back up into shape. It literally whipped by me as I ran, stinging my legs and arms. I felt like I deserved it for leaving Daisy alone. By the time I reached the tree, I was breathless and shaking but still determined.

Luckily, in the woods, the passage of a dozen heavily laden horses is not easily lost. The forest floor was churned up, right down to the mud still under the leaves from last night's downpour. The trees seemed to echo with the din of their passing as I slid and slithered along their track. Even under the eternal gloaming of the interwoven branches, it was a clear trail to follow.

Then it turned and began to climb higher onto stonier ground. The first shelf it reached, I paused. Here, in the first place a little clearer of trees, I finally noticed that the sun was going down, its long light laying in slanting bars, dwindling away. I felt a quick, short stab of fear. Once it got dark, I was sure to lose the track, if I didn't find my quarry before. I picked up my pace.

I had a slim hope that the height and narrowness of the path would tire the horses and slow down the troop, but I was starting to get weary, too. I hadn't eaten anything since our oatmeal breakfast, and had run, I reckoned, about ten miles, some of it up the mountain side, carrying a gun that seemed to weigh like an anchor in my arms.

I stopped at last, stymied, on a rocky cliff. There were three paths the kidnappers might have gone: up, down, and straight ahead, and no clue at all which they had taken on the stony ground. As I stood, bewildered, trying to choose which way to go, the last light of the setting sun failed, and I was left in gloom as black as my sudden despair. I bowed my head and leaned on the rifle as if it were the only thing to keep me upright. And I prayed: prayed for help, prayed for forgiveness, prayed for guidance, somehow, through the lost wilderness.

A light sprang up in the heart of the murky abyss ahead. I peered, unbelieving. Someone had lit a campfire a ways off, and its red light, though tiny, gleamed like a beacon, a goal to head for in the chartless dark. My heart gushed thankfulness, and I made sure to inform the Almighty, briefly, of my gratitude.

The light looked to me like it was dancing a little below, so I took the sloping lower path. It was slow, nevertheless, because I had to part feel my way down, cautious foot by cautious foot. I didn't want to alert anyone of my approach, or fall down and injure myself. I fervently wished for moonrise but knew that wasn't till the later hours of the night. It was about an hour, therefore, before I reached the outmost verge of the campfire and peeked carefully from the bushes.

I had caught up with the MacCallister Gang.

"I don't like it. I don't like these woods at all."

"Don't fret, Dolly m'dear." The Captain laid a comforting arm on his lady's shoulders. "Tomorrow, we'll be on the other side of the mountain and safely back at headquarters."

"One hears stories, you know. Nasty, disquieting stories." She brooded a bit. "And what about the girl?"

"Yes. Check and see if she's ready to capitulate, Joe."

Grisly Joe was sitting by the fire and nursing something simmering in a pot. He stood up and dashed the ladle down with a clank, turning to the fringe of the forest surrounding the camp.

There was Daisy, still glowering, still clutching the jar tightly, tied to a tree with a length of rope around her middle. It seemed to be just long enough for her to sit down and stand up. Joe sidled over to her, eyes never leaving her, hand stretched out to take the little barrel.

Daisy jumped up, screeching and kicking and chomping her teeth, for all the world like a dog protecting its yard at the end of its tether. Grisly Joe leaped back to safety. It seems he had learned caution.

"No, sir," he said. "I don't think she's give up yet."

"Damn it all, the child has spirit," the Captain exclaimed. Then an idea seemed to strike him. He turned to Mrs. MacCallister.

"I say, my love, have you ever considered having a daughter?"

Even from where I crouched, I could see the lady's cheeks redden under her face powder.

"Richard MacCallister, if you think that at my time of life—and in our line of work—that I could be having an infant hanging off me, well, you have another think coming!"

"But consider, Dolly, we have before us a girl of indomitable courage and reserve, with all the hard parts of having a child—birth and raising and so on—already taken care of! Think of the asset she could be to our merry band, wiggling through windows and opening locks from inside, doing the wash, deceiving the hardest hearts through her apparent harmlessness!"

"You mean adoption?" Mrs. MacCallister sounded dubious, but perhaps coming around. She looked towards Daisy with an assessing eye.

"Two birds with one stone. What else can we do with her? We could turn this little *contretemps* into a triumph. Billy, come here."

The gangling old man ambled over from where he had been tending the horses. Captain MacCallister poured out a bowl of soup.

"Give this to our young guest. She seems hungry."

Billy took up the bowl and carried it happily straight to Daisy. She looked at him warily. He just smiled back. After a second, she snatched the soup away and started gulping it down. The old man went back to his horses.

The bandits watched until she had finished the entire bowl, the couple with a sort of sickly-sweet smirk, the large black man kindly, and Grisly Joe like he resented every swallow. Finally, she set the bowl down.

"Thank you," she said.

"Are you feeling better, dear?" asked the lady in ingratiating, simpering tones. "You see, we're not such bad people, after all, are we?"

"Yes, you are," said Daisy calmly. "I heard you talkin', and don't think just `cause I'm little I don't understand. No thank you, I already got a Ma and Pa, and I don't mean to trade `em for worse, `specially no-good rotten thieves."

Captain MacCallister choked, and Mrs. MacCallister huffed up like a toad. Grisly Joe squinted at them through red eyes.

"Now?" he asked tightly. "Kin I do it now?"

"No, you can't," said Sugar, walking forward into the light. "Cap'n, we got to take that child back. We can't take her to the hideout `cause she'd knew where we hid. We can't leave her in the woods, she'd most likely die. We got to take her back, and if nobody else don't want to do it, I will."

MacCallister looked up at him in alarm.

"Now, Sugar, you know you can't do that. What if they catch you? You're a runaway, and if anyone finds you, they'll take you right back, you know they will. Ever since you came to the Territory, the only safe place for you is running with my company. You'll stay right here with us."

Now, I knew this was a lie. In those days, any slave that made it to the Territory was automatically free, and nobody could make him do what he didn't want to. My blood boiled to think of this bandit taking advantage of that friendly man. I seethed in the bushes and wondered what I could do.

I had one shot. The minute I used it, even if I killed one of the gang, the rest would be on me like chickens on a June bug. If I shot the Captain, Joe would get me for sure. There didn't seem any point in targeting Mrs. MacCallister or Daft Billy, and I certainly didn't want to kill Sugar, who seemed the most innocent of the lot. When it got right down to it, I really didn't want to kill anybody, not even Grisly Joe.

"Sugar, I swear on my honor as a gentleman and a highwayman, we'll find some way out without harming this little girl," MacCallister declaimed, hand uplifted. "And you know how I hold my honor dear."

The rest of the gang looked solemn at that. I could see that they believed him. Even under all his strutting and posturing, I could see that *he* believed it, that he was serious about this image he had of himself, and the honor that went with it. And, suddenly, I knew what I could do.

I straightened up, and took a firm grip on my rifle. I marched out of the dark bushes and into the light, to the astonishment of the surprised gang.

"Captain MacCallister," I said.

I gathered my courage.

"I challenge you to a duel."

Chapter Six:
Dueling Tales

There are three different versions about what happened next. Let me show you the one that got written down in a book first. Here's how that one goes:

"Out of the shadows stepped a grim young man, his deadly iron pointed at the Captain's heart. The camp was thrown into confusion. Who was this, and how had he discovered the intrepid group in the wilderness? His clothes were torn and his eyes savage but, still, there was an air of breeding about him that hinted at one more gently raised.

"Captain MacCallister rose slowly and strode forward with a calm step until the barrel of the youth's gun was inches from his breast, a breast whose heart beat steadily, unchanged by the death standing before it.

"Who are you, lad," he said sturdily, "To be challenging me?"

"I am Robert Bellamy," came the reply, "And that is my sister Marigold that you have carried away. I've come to claim her and vengeance against her captors."

"Young man, assuage your fury and let cooler heads prevail, lest your rash actions lead you to an unfortunate fate. 'Twas no fault of ours," the Captain replied in a fatherly tone. "By her own actions and choice, she came with the company. Even now we were discussing how to safely return her."

"You lie," the youth in his frenzy spat, and in that moment, sealed the destiny that followed. MacCallister drew back, stung. The lie direct is a challenge that no gentleman can ignore, whichever way his finer nature or benevolent instincts might incline. In that moment, his blood turned to iced water in his veins, his resolve to steel.

His beautiful lady, sensing the outrage to his exalted spirit, came rushing to his side, pouring entreaties into his ear.

"Do not do it, my love," she pleaded. "There is something fatal in yon boy. Please, please, for the sake of your own Dorothea, shun this deadly conflict!"

"The challenge is met," the Captain sternly replied, his eyes never leaving the foolish young man. "May God have mercy on your soul."

The lady fell away from his bosom in despair. His loyal crew, manlier in their resolve, saluted his decision with loud huzzahs. MacCallister forthwith set them to preparing the theater where the ill-starred act should be played out."

Did you ever hear such an old load of balderdash in all your days? The writer couldn't even get my sister's name right. And he keeps skittering around the fact that I was all of twelve-years-old. Now, here's how I remember it.

When I stepped into the light, the whole gang jumped like

cats in a room full of rockers, even the bold Captain MacCallister. The next moment, Grisly Joe had pulled a brace of wicked-looking long knives, Sugar was holding a rusty Brown Bess that looked like a twig in his hands, and Mrs. MacCallister held a little lady's handgun in an unsure grip.

MacCallister hadn't pulled his own pistol. He stood blinking at me a moment, then raised his hands. Not up in surrender, you understand, but palm outward, in a calming, shushing gesture. He didn't march up to me, but he did come forward a few steps. He was weaving back and forth with each step, trying, I imagine, to get out of my firing sight. I kept the muzzle pointing whichever way he turned. Finally, he stopped.

"Easy, easy, son. That gun is dangerous. Let's not have any accidents. Who are you, and what do you want with us then? We don't have a lot of money."

"Only what you've stolen, I guess. I'm Bob Bellamy, and that was my house you robbed, and that's my sister, Daisy, you've kidnapped!"

"Well, we didn't want to." He grimaced. "In fact, we were just discussing how to get rid— I mean, get her back safely."

"Like fun you were. I heard you talking about making her a thief like yourself." I took a firmer grip on the rifle. "That's why I challenge you, you slippery snake. For my sister, and if I win, for your gang to let us both leave this place safely."

His lady came flouncing up to his side. She leaned in behind him to whisper in his ear. I mean, I guess she thought she was whispering, but like a lot of loud-mouthed people, she must have thought she was being quieter and more secretive than she was. I could hear her pretty plain.

"Richard, you've got to accept this challenge. If you back down from fighting a scrawny little boy, how long do you think you'll have the respect of your men? And look at him, he can barely hold that rifle! How good a shot do you think he could be? It's unpleasant I know, but HE challenged YOU. It's not your fault if you have to bag him. In fact, honor demands it, my dear."

I could see him standing a little straighter after each point of her encouragement, though doubt seemed to linger in his expression, pulling the corners of his mouth down and tightening his eyes.

"What do you think, boys?" he called over his shoulder. For a moment, the gang seemed taken aback that their opinion should be polled by their leader. Even Daft Billy, who had wandered over to taste the soup bubbling over fire, looked up puzzled at MacCallister's question. But one was already smelling blood.

"Yeah, drop the little runt quick, so we can get out of here," said Grisly Joe eagerly. He grinned. "Don't worry. If you just wing him, I'll finish him off for you." He clashed his knives together with a sliding *zing*. "Save a little powder and shot."

"I guess you got to do it, boss, it bein' ya honor and all," said Sugar glumly. "I just wish you didn' have to it in front of the little girl. Her bein' his sister an' like that."

MacCallister gulped. I was the only one to see it, being in the position I was in. He was trapped. His expression said it was all very well for everybody to say he should fight the duel, but it was he who would actually be the one in danger. But there was no way out.

Then he stood up completely straight and accepted it. If this would have to be done, he would play it out, up to the hilt.

"Young man, I accept your challenge," he said grandly. He poised like a tragedian on stage. "The winner shall take your sister away, and none—" he looked at me hard—"shall interfere."

It struck me right then that I might well be facing death. You'd think it would have been obvious, but I seriously hadn't been thinking about it in those terms. I had sort of hoped to wing the Captain and trust him to honor his agreement. Or at worst, he'd wing me (not wanting to kill a child), and then they'd run off with Daisy. Then I'd have done everything I could. The thought that I might be dead at the end of all this, possibly after the attention of Joe and his knives, made me suddenly sick.

Oh well, I thought. *At least then I won't have to face Mother with an explanation.* Perhaps God will be more forgiving than she would be, faced with the disappearance of her daughter.

Captain MacCallister turned on his heel and faced his people, hands raised.

"This shall all be done according to the rules," he announced. "No one is to interfere between us, and no matter the outcome, the conditions must be met. Let all of you witness, for the record, that I am guiltless in this fellow's fate."

He turned to Sugar.

"You. You hold the girl by that tree." He indicated a spot halfway between us. "Mr. Bellamy and I shall start from there, pace ten, and fire. Should he win, release her, and let her join her brother."

He turned to me, lip curled, a far-off dreamy expression in his eyes.

"Mr. Bellamy, will you join me? You may raise your gun, sir. You are safe for now. The rest of you, stay by the fire."

The big black man gingerly untied Daisy and led her to the spot. She endured it haughtily and walked over with him without a struggle, money jar still clanking in her grip. She drew up to where MacCallister and I had approached each other cautiously.

"Bob," she said, "this may be the stupidest thing you ever done."

"Yeah," I said. "I know it."

Now, I'm going to tell you what Daisy said happened, as she saw it.

"So, when I saw you step out of the woods and say you wanted to fight a duel, I thought right then that that was the most foolish idea I ever heard. Useless too. I was doing fine.

"You thought you had to do it? I didn't. I was going to get away from those idiots one way or another. There was a dozen ways. I bet I could have run off in the woods when I had to do my business, or talked that old softy Sugar into lettin' me escape, or squirmed out of that rope. I was workin' on that one already. You ever know any knot that would hold me?

"But there you were with this duel idea. He wasn't holdin' me very tight, but I knew if I ran away then, they'd prolly just shoot you and be done with it, so I couldn't do nothin'.

"I have to say you looked mighty pale through the whole deal. You were sweatin' bad and holding the gun too tight. Remember Pa tellin' you loose, light, and firm? I wanted to remind you but, suddenly I couldn't talk, somehow. I didn't want anything bad to happen to you. The only thing that come out was how stupid you were."

Myself, I was finding it hard to think of anything right then, even of Daisy much, and certainly not what we should do next if I won. I was transfixed on what was happening. I looked hard at MacCallister and wondered if we might come to some sort of mutual agreement to call off the fight. But now he was off in his own little world.

"You shall turn and lower your rifle when the count reaches ten," he said. "And I shall draw my pistol. Then we shall see who is quick, and who has entered history."

He smirked.

"I fear that whatever happens, you shall be but a footnote to my tale. My legend shall be…legendary," he finished lamely. He smoothed over it hurriedly.

"Now, back to back. Say your final prayers. And let the count begin. Will you do the honors, my dear?"

"Yes, my dearest." Mrs. MacCallister turned her gaze heavenwards, eyelashes fluttering like butterflies trapped in a cobweb. "And may flights of angels guard thee!"

She bowed her head and looked to be praying for quite a dramatic pause, then lifted her head.

"One," she enunciated, clear and eager.

I took a step. Now that the entire gang was behind me, with the Captain starting to get farther away from standing between us, my back was starting to itch.

"Two."

Would MacCallister's honor be enough to keep him from simply shooting me in the back? My shoulder blades started to squirm.

"Three."

The forest in front of me seemed dark and impenetrable outside the light of the fire. I looked down at my feet. The grass, the leaves, the twigs, were suddenly very clear and delineated. I could see each blade. They seemed very dear in their individuality.

"Four."

The gang. Would the gang really refrain from some

underhandedness? Dolly MacCallister's voice was starting to sound a little strained. I thought about her little pistol, and it now didn't seem so negligible. There was a decided burning feeling growing on my back.

"Five."

And Grisly Joe. I could imagine any perfidy coming from his hands. Even if I won, could I be sure he wouldn't just go wild and chop me up? I listened to the crackle of the fire and imagined him sneaking stealthily behind.

"Six."

I tried to put these things out of my mind and think about what to do if I was somehow triumphant. I'd drop the gun, which was a shame, but after it was discharged, it would be useless and heavy. I'd head for Daisy and hope that she'd head for me, then it'd be straight off into the woods.

"Seven."

There was now a definite burning hole where I was imagining a bullet or a knife plunging between my shoulders. The rest of my body felt like ice. Sweating ice.

"Eight!"

The old bag was getting keyed up, I thought angrily. The numbers were coming quicker now, I was sure, and I deeply resented it. Each little sliver of time was getting precious to me.

"Nine!"

I'd never noticed before just how much the woods looked like a church, with the trees like pillars and their branches like a roof. A church that went on forever. I looked up and could see one star through the woven branches.

"Ten!"

I turned, lowered my gun, and fired. For a moment, all was blur and brightness.

I'm going to tell you what Daisy saw. I didn't see it myself. This is what she told me happened.

She said that during the countdown, around five, Grisly Joe had started up, but Billy had held him back, shaking his head. He tried to shrug the old man off, but Mrs. MacCallister cut him a sharp glance. He backed down, snarling.

Daisy could feel Sugar's hands slacking as his attention got wound up with each pace. She was ready, whatever happened, to break away and run. She tried not to tense up. That would alert the big man, give him a clue what she was up to.

The Captain seemed to be a hundred miles away, or like he was in a theater box, watching himself as he was moving across a stage. Daisy looked at me and saw I was stiff, yet somehow trembling. It came her mind that in this state, the man might very easily and very calmly shoot me dead. She felt like screaming, if only to break the tension, but was afraid what that might do.

Instead, she concentrated on me. It might be the last minute she would ever see me alive. And that's why she saw what she did.

Right on ten, as I wheeled around, she was just near enough to see a shadowy figure rise out of the bushes behind me. It was dark, and all she could see was a buckskin coat, the fringe shaking with the abrupt movement, a broad-brimmed hat that hid the face in shadow, and the long musket firing at the exact time as my rifle went off.

The Captain clutched his chest. The quickly-drawn pistol now held in his hand shot at the sky as he squeezed it convulsively. The gang around the fire lunged forward, Dolly with a cry, Joe with a curse. Daft Billy leapt right over the fire, knocking over the kettle as he did, spilling the soup and dousing the flames. In the light of the dying embers, Daisy shot towards me, free of Sugar's hold as he rushed to his fallen leader.

I stood in a haze of powder smoke, stunned a bit. I dropped the gun from my numbed hand. Daisy appeared out of the cloud, braids flying, jar jingling with each furiously pumping step. She grabbed my arm.

"Come on, come on! We've got to get out of here, fast!" Behind her, the babble of the gang was growing, like a cracked hornet's nest. I could hear Mrs. MacCallister wailing like a banshee.

I jerked out of my daze and took Daisy's hand. I tried to lead her, in a vague way, to where I recalled entering the clearing, but she tugged me right into the trees where we were standing, and then we were just running, running away into the dark woods.

In seconds, it was pitch black once more. After a while, I don't know that I could have found our way back even if I wanted to. We held our hands like grim death so we wouldn't lose each other in the dark, though I might have been able to locate Daisy by the clanking of the coins.

"Is there any way you can hold that quieter?" I whispered angrily as we stumbled hurriedly along. "What if somebody hears that and follows us?"

"If you have any ideas how to do it, trot 'em out," gasped Daisy. "Ow! That's a bush you're trying to drag me through."

"That jar's ringing like a bell!"

"If you're worried about noise," she panted, "Why don't you just shut up? Ow!"

I tugged her out of the bush.

"Oh, come on!"

We seethed side by side in silence for a while. Now and then, one or the other of us would slide or stumble, and we'd help each other up. Eventually, I stopped worrying about pursuit. My heart, despite the running, was finally starting to beat more regularly again, my pulse steadier. I could breathe. And think. My brain stopped whirling over the duel and began thinking about the consequences.

We stopped when my foot plunked into a shallow brook. I pulled Daisy after me, but she was able to hop right over it with the impetus of my own fall. I stepped back out, shaking my foot.

"Let's rest," I panted. I took a few paces upstream. "Get a drink."

"Okay," she said.

We knelt down by the trickle and caught our breath. I cupped my hand and pulled up a sample of water, sniffing it. All I could smell was the acrid whiff of gunpowder.

I let it drizzle off and rinsed my fingers, and tried again. The smell was less, and I sniffed again. Finally, I tried a lick.

"It seems okay," I said. For the next few minutes, we were cupping and slurping from the little stream. When our thirst was finally satisfied, we sat back, quiet for a moment.

"So," said Daisy. "Did you find anything to eat when you were out?"

I was speechless. When I spoke at last, I almost shrieked.

"What?" I looked away, then back to where I could just see her pale blonde hair glowing in the dark. "Are you serious? After all this, after facing death and being lost the Almighty knows where in the dead of night, that is what you ask about?"

"Well, I'm hungry. First things first."

I collapsed, incredulous.

"Nuts," I said. "I found some nuts. And no, I don't have any with me."

"That's too bad." A pause. "You know, Ma's not going to be happy about you losing Pa's rifle."

"Unhappy about losing a rifle? Is that all? You know, don't you, that I just killed a man?"

"I don't think you did."

"You don't?" I considered for a bit. "You think he might still be alive then?"

"I didn't say that."

I gave up and looked around, trying to think of something else. I realized I could see Daisy a little clearer in the gloom. The light was better. *The moon,* I thought. The moon is getting ready to rise, and this is its glow, creeping over the horizon.

"Come on," I said, and heaved myself to my feet. "Let's see if we can see where we are. We need to find a clear spot we can look out from."

"Can't we rest a little longer?"

"No, the moon's coming up."

"So? If we wait, it'll be brighter."

"Daisy, I don't want to waste any time at all. If we can spot any clue at all to the way home, it will be from a high spot when the moon is brightest."

"But I'm tired!"

"You think I'm not? I've been running, and you been riding, at least part of the way, and you're up on me by one bowl of soup."

"But, Bob..." she started, then stopped. I could hear the sudden misery in her voice. I thought, like I was just remembering, that she was six. Sometimes she talked so sturdily I forgot.

"I tell you what," I said kindly. "I'll carry you pick-a-back for a ways, how 'bout that? Then you can rest, and we can get a move on at the same time."

"'Kay," she sniffled. I reached my hand out, and we stood up.

"Bob?" she said. "I'm glad you came for me. And that you didn't get killed."

"Well," I said with grim chuckle, "the night is still young." I crouched in preparation to take her up.

"What's that?" she squeaked.

I went tense. I'd heard it, too. Something like an almost noiseless step, and the crackle of crunched leaves. My eyes puckered against the darkness, searching. Then a tall shadow detached itself from the outline of a tree. Daisy gasped. I reached for my sling and cursed myself when I realized I didn't have any more stones.

The tall figure approached with implacable steps, not seeming to care about stealth any longer. At last, it loomed over us, not three feet from where we stood frozen on the spot. I put Daisy behind me, one of her hands clamped to mine, the other still clutching the jar snatched up from the brook's side. The figure raised its hand.

There was a *clank* and a *hiss*, and a small flame sprang revealed from a dark lantern, blinding with its surprising light.

I held my hand up, squinting against the brightness. There, looking grimly down on us, was Old Thunder.

Chapter Seven:
What Thunder Said

We looked at each other in silence. The light cast half of his craggy face in shadow. Out of that shadow, eyes glinted as he seemed to study us slowly where we huddled together. Finally, he lowered the light.

"Children," he said. "White children." He relaxed just a shade. It was only then I noticed how tense he had been. It suddenly seemed to me that he was very tired.

I looked even closer. His buckskins were dusty and torn, streaked with trailing green, and his moccasins dark with fresh mud.

"What are you doing out here?" he asked wearily.

I decided to be a little cautious and stall a bit. No telling what a stranger's attitude might be, finding two vulnerable youngsters at their mercy, as it were.

"Hello, mister. I'm Bob Bellamy, and this is my sister, Daisy."

"H'llo," said Daisy. He lifted one hand in a sketch of greeting, raised the tiniest corner of his mouth as if to indicate a smile. These instantly dropped back to a questioning puzzlement.

"We're a little out of our path," I said, feeling my way through what I should say. "We were out here with a party of folks and got separated. Could you direct us back towards Cumberton?"

"Cumberton," he mumbled. "No, you cannot go that way."

"We don't want to go all the way to town," Daisy piped up. "We just want to get back to our cabin up the mountain."

He went still.

"The cabin? The Deacon's cabin? Near the stream called Tears-of-the Mountain?"

"It's near a stream," I admitted cautiously, "but *we* are settling in there now."

"No, we must not go there till the sun is high, and I would not go back that way at night."

He pondered for a moment, then came to a decision.

"You children must come with me." He started off abruptly at a great pace, striding with his long legs into the dark. Daisy and I, startled, were drawn after in his wake, almost by instinct.

"Hey!" said Daisy. "Not so fast! We're tired!"

The big man chuckled grimly, a rumble in his throat.

"Little woman, until you have been running every night for two seasons, you do not know tired."

"Where are we going?" I asked.

"Deeper into the woods," he answered. "Even I do not go to these places often, boy. So, we must have respect and walk with care."

"Well, speaking with respect, Mr. Thunder, I don't think

my sister can go much farther on her own, and my name is Bob Bellamy, not boy."

He stopped and turned back to us. He studied us closely again in the lamp's tiny flame.

"And my name is not Thunder, but those who do not know me call me that."

He turned to Daisy.

"Little woman, I ask your forgiveness. I did not see how weary you truly were." He bent down, looking in her face gently. She looked up at his, squinting a little past the hair hanging in her face. One of her pigtails had come undone in our flight, the ribbon lost somewhere.

"May I lift you on my shoulders and carry you a ways?" he asked gravely.

Daisy smiled a little wanly.

"I would be much obliged, sir."

Daisy looked at the jar in her hands.

"Just a minute."

She turned away and fumbled around. When she turned back the canister was rather obviously stowed away under her blouse. She held her arms out in readiness.

"Hold this, Bob Bellamy." He handed me the lantern. I took it carefully. The hood was hot. The Indian stooped down and picked Daisy up. With a swirl of skirts, she was up on his back.

"Hang on tight, little woman," he said, "but do not choke me. I will need my hands. The lantern, Bob Bellamy."

I passed it back to him, and without a word, we were moving again, although I noticed at a slightly slower pace than before. Whether it was because of his new burden or that he was taking it easier on me, I don't know, but I was grateful for it.

After a little while, Daisy spoke up.

"So, what is your name then, if it's not Thunder?" she asked.

He walked forward silently a bit. Finally, he answered.

"Thunder is part of my name. You may call me Thunder, for now." A considering pause. "Later, perhaps, I might tell you the whole of my name."

"Fair enough," I put in. Since he was talking, I decided to ask a question.

"Tell me, Mr. Thunder, why are *you* out here in the woods? Hunting?"

Again, a grim dry chuckle, almost a grunt.

"As you say. But I am the one that is hunted, and I am the one who flees."

"Somethin' after you?" said Daisy. She sounded a little breathless from up on top of her jostling perch. "What is it, a bear? Is it behind us?"

"Don't be silly, Daisy," I said. "Somebody after you, Thunder?"

"Yes."

Another silence.

"Who is it? The law?"

A longer silence. Then he answered, in a low voice that I could scarce hear over the rattle of the leaves under our feet.

"It is the one they call the Deacon."

"You mean Jerimoth Whitley?" I raised my voice, surprised. He hissed.

"Do not speak it aloud!" he said angrily. "It will help him find us!"

"But he's dead," said Daisy. "We saw his tomb. He's dead."

"Yes," said Thunder. "That is what makes him so dangerous."

That shut us up. For a while, the only sounds were the calling of birds, the wind shushing through the tops of the trees, and the slap and swish of our passage through brush and leaves. I had been a little assured by Thunder's kindness before, but now I was knocked back by what he was saying.

It wasn't that I thought he was insane exactly, not unbalanced or anything like that. But, apparently, he had some crazy ideas, and Pa had warned me that people with odd beliefs were liable to act on them in unpredictable ways. He explained that to me after old Mrs. Bascombe had subjected me to a forcible baptism one afternoon.

I mean it's one thing for a little kid to imagine ghosts in dark corners of the room, and quite another for a grown man (albeit a primitive, the thought came to me sneakily) living in the workaday world to base his actions on the idea that a dead man was chasing him.

I cleared my throat.

"So," I started, "why is he after you? Some job you didn't finish for him or something?"

I couldn't see much of his lumbering frame in the dark, but I could almost feel him grow tense, offended by my question.

"Only I heard you were his servant," I added lamely.

"I was never his servant," he said tightly. "We worked together for a time."

His footsteps thudded a few paces, then he added, with bitter wistfulness:

"In the beginning, I was his friend."

And with a last thrashing, we were out of the woods and on the bare mountainside. We had come much higher than I had realized. We were held as in a little cup between the trees below us, the mountain black above us, and the line of rolling hills to our left. After the dim forest, the starlight and incipient moon-rise made details strikingly plain.

For one thing, I could see how gaunt and tired Thunder really was. The lines in his face were etched in faint shadow.

He blew out the lantern and pointed to an outcrop of rock ahead and above us.

"We will rest there," he announced, "and I will tell you how it was."

We staggered up to the place, a gritty incline that could only be called a path by a considerable stretch of the imagination. There were times when I was on my hands and knees and the ground was almost in my face. When we reached it, it was a tiny shelf. Two boulders, one taller and one shorter, made a natural seat.

Slowly, tiredly, but with great care, Thunder lifted Daisy from around his neck and set her down, and then bent himself to sit on the stone. Daisy and I sank to the ground at his feet. I think we had the better place; it was softer. We all sat, catching our breath.

When we were breathing easier, Thunder reached inside his fringed buckskin and took out a pouch, and from that, he took what looked like two old strips of leather.

"Here. Eat it. It will give you strength." He handed them to us.

"What is it?" asked Daisy, nose wrinkling. She held it like it was a dried toad.

"It is good. It is meat." He looked at her expression. "Do you have so much food with you that you can cast it away?"

That was a thought, and we certainly were hungry. I took a bite, and it was hard enough getting a chaw off. Daisy followed suit when she saw that I didn't fall over right away. It was rough going and an exercise in chewing, but once it got started, it tasted good and was mighty grateful to an empty stomach.

Soon, we were gnawing thoughtlessly away and hardly noticed when Thunder started his tale.

"The Deacon came," he began quietly, "many seasons ago. At that time, most of my people were gone into the earth, but there were still a few of us…"

"Killed off?" asked Daisy matter-of-factly through a mouthful of jerky. "Was there a fight?"

"No. There was a sickness that went before the white people, and we had no power—no medicine—before it. I was speaker for my folk, but I knew not how to speak to it. I tried speaking to it in herbs, in dances, by messengers, in the Long Words, but it was smoke before the wind. Many died. I came near to the shadows myself.

"By the time the sickness passed, Cumberton was planted at the foot of the mountain, and white people walked much of our land, and more every year. One came to the town, but not to stay there, but because it was at the very edge of what they call the wild lands. I found him wandering the hills where the last of us had withdrawn.

"He was… He did not know how to live in the wild places. He was very near to death when I found him, starving, sick, and talking like a fool. I thought about letting him die. What had the white people done for me? But he was very low, and miserable, and I was a speaker still.

"So, I fed him, and cared for him, and spoke life into him again. And when he was once more healed and whole, he sat up and thanked me and said he had at last found what he had been seeking."

"What was he looking for?" I asked.

"This is how he told it to me. He was born in the land over the water, from where all the white men come. There was a big town, many times the size of Cumberton, and there he went to learn in a lodge where their wise men gather to learn and talk knowledge, about stars and plants and animals and the earth and the tales of long ago."

"You mean a college?"

"As you say. That was his word. He said there was much talk but little wisdom, as it seemed to him. There was much how and what, but little why. Always, he looked for the why. He said he thought he had found it, at last, in the words of a wise man named New Tun."

"New-Newton? Isaac Newton, the scientist?"

"Yes. He often spoke this name and that word. He studied this man's work in the lodge and drank in his teaching but, always, it seemed that the wisdom he sought was just beyond. So, he went to this man's old home in search of more learning, and he found it in hidden writing and old books. And he learned a secret, as he thought."

Thunder paused and thought a bit.

"I am not sure how to tell this thing to you, but I will try. He said the lore they taught in the lodge was like the law they had written: it told you how things should work, and that if you tried otherwise than the law, there was punishment. You could not jump from a height and expect to fly. You fell. They taught that the law did this of itself. But the old wisdom, the wisdom this Newton sought, said that there were persons—powers— spirits that were the ones behind the laws, upholding them. And if they were persons, then they could be forced or pleased into changing the law for those that threatened or paid them.

"He went back to the lodge and tried there to tell his brothers this thing that he had rediscovered, this thing one of their greatest chiefs had explored. But they laughed at him and drove him out, saying their science had grown beyond these thoughts. He went away to follow these thoughts alone, and his heart burned inside him.

"He decided the land he came from was too old, used up and bound down by the laws, and by the rules of the churchmen. He decided to come here, a land he thought of as new, despite all the long years we have been here. He would find the powers, wild and free, and he would ride them, whether as friend or master."

"He sounds like a cuckoo-bird," said Daisy sleepily. She had finished her jerky and was starting to rock to and fro a bit. Every time she almost fell over, she would catch herself and be wide awake for a moment, and then start rocking again.

"He sounds like some kind of wizard," I said, determined to hold up Western learning. "It's no wonder he was kicked out of college. Seems like a load of old bosh, if you ask me."

Thunder frowned and looked down at me from a great height.

"He was not altogether wrong," he said. "Had I not spoken life into him? I had pleaded with the spirits for him, and they had heard me. I found truth in his words and knew much that he told me, though changed and told strangely. And in one great way, I knew he was a fool. But he begged me to teach him."

He sighed and unbent a little.

"Perhaps I was the fool. But my people were gone, and I am old, and I am lonely. And I agreed.

"I told him all the old tales, and taught him the long songs, and showed him the sacred places. One night, under a new moon, we mingled blood and became brothers. Together, we built his house at the foot of the mountain, as a strong place and a marker. And we said that beyond that, by our words, no other white man would ever go into the farther lands."

"Well, that was kind of selfish," I said. "Plenty of space up here for all kinds of folks." I looked back down at the woods. "If you like this sort of place." I shivered a bit. A quiet little wind was creeping up out of the trees.

"Yes," he admitted simply. "I did not tell myself that, but I was. I was wounded and angry, and his anger fed mine. Our word went through the wood, and the people huddled in their town. But he was in that one thing a fool, as I said, and I fell in that thing after him."

"What was that?"

He exhaled sharply, a sound between a sigh and a groan of pain.

"You cannot order the spirits. You plead, you beg, you bargain, you may even joke with them, so they do something for you as a jest, but you do not command. You may only ride along with the Powers. You cannot drive Them. He—the Deacon—stood on a high place and tried to command a destruction on the people below. The destruction was thrown back upon him, and he was cast down."

"Serve him right," murmured Daisy.

"Even then, he was not dead. Even then, I tried to save him. But I could not speak for him again. Everything turned a deaf ear to my pleadings. I hoped that if he yet lived, he might learn and grow wise. I could not speak life into him. His life and mine were now one.

"Still, he lingered in pain and would not die but could not

live. At last, I said to him there was no hope. I offered to sing the Last Song for him, to ease his passing and guard his way into the other world. And then my foolishness was revealed. He laughed at it.

"He told me that he would not, could not truly die. Though his heart ceased and his breath fled and his flesh be buried, he would rise and walk again, and it was all thanks to me, his brother in blood.

"'Even now I take your life, and it feeds me, though it spills out again, like water flowing through a gourd with a hole,' he said. 'But when death is full come, the hole will close. Then I shall rise and take all your life, and it will fill me once more.'

"'And me? What of me, then?' I asked.

"He laughed again. 'Then I will sing the Last Song for you, my brother.'

"I fled from him. In some fashion, I have been fleeing him since.

"But I went back, when at last I felt him die, and buried him in the tomb we had prepared. I sealed it well and sat to wait and watch."

"I wouldn't have done that," I said. "I'd have ripped that skunk to pieces and seen if he could raise up like that, or burned him up to ash."

"I could not. We were blood of blood. There is a test when one has appeared to pass away, but there is doubt. I put a knife to his chest and sought to open a vein. But when I began, I felt the blade on my own heart. I cannot destroy him, or harm him with my hands.

"So, I sealed him away and watched. When the sun set that evening, when the last glow had faded, and the true dark had fallen, he came. Out of the rock and stone, he stepped like they were mist. His eyes did not blink, his chest did not heave, but his footfall on the steps was solid and earthy, and he pushed the hemlock back where he passed.

"He took the last step down and turned to look where I stood. He smiled a hungry smile and reached out an arm.

"'It was good of you to wait,' he said. I turned and ran, like the deer than hears the wolf.

"For two seasons I have run, and he always follows. He is not fast, but he never tires, and he never stops, and he always knows where I am. By morning, he is in his tomb again, and then I can sleep. But I grow weaker and weaker. When the snow comes again, I do not think I will run anymore."

"Why don't you go away?" asked Daisy. Thunder's tale had snapped her out of her sleepies, and she was wide awake now. "Get far away, too far for him to reach from his tomb."

He shook his head.

"The boundaries that drive people away also keep me in. The power we wove together holds me fenced in this land, and he hunts me across it. My own hands have made this cage, and I flutter to and fro in it."

"Now, I don't quite see that," I said. "After all, Ma and us moved in here, right into the Deacon's cabin, and no magic hoodoo has kicked us out."

"Hasn't it, Bob Bellamy? Has the house welcomed you? Has the land been soft and your luck good? Why are you left alone, lured into the woods, if not to destroy you?"

I thought about it, thought about the storm, and the ruined flour, and the bandits, and every effort going astray. Then about the Indian finding us and bringing us up to this high place. My heart sank.

"Is that it, Mr. Thunder? Have *you* brought us here to

destroy us?"

"No, no. My spirit is not so crooked." He looked taken aback by the suspicion. "I seek to keep you safe."

"Seems to me he's after you, Mister Thunder," said Daisy. "I'm thinkin' we'd be safer on our own."

"Yes, he follows me, little woman. But if he finds two lost and weary children in the woods, I do not think he will pat them on the head and let them go their way." He made two snatching moves with a clawed hand. "How, how, two little bites, and he goes on his way refreshed."

He stood up.

"Come," he said. "We must move on."

The wind, which had been growing stealthily, burst out of the trees below in a pouncing gust, scattering rattling leaves before it. Daisy jumped up with a squeal and clutched Thunder's leg. I looked fearfully down.

Under the black branches flickered a dim green glow, like a rotten fish, but growing brighter. I wanted to run but stood transfixed. Even Thunder seemed unable to move, as if overcome with dread recognition. Then the branches parted and the gaunt, black-robed figure of Deacon Whitley stepped out. He stood there a moment, wreathed in cold silent green flame, and looked up at us with bleak, unblinking eyes. He took a step forward.

"It was good of you," he rasped, "To wait for me."

Chapter Eight:
Onari

Thunder jumped off the side of the mountain. I thought for a moment he had decided to escape death at the hands of the Deacon by leaping over the stony seat into the yawning void, but the next instant, his head rose up over the rock, arms outstretched to us.

"Come!" he commanded.

Daisy and I didn't need to be invited twice. The Deacon's unflagging tread had already brought his rotting green light halfway up the slope to us. We grabbed Thunder's ropy arms like they were a life-line, and he yanked us up and over the boulder. And like that, we were on the other side of the mountain, looking down into an unknown valley.

I only had the briefest time to take it in. The moon had already risen over the low hills here, turning the trees into a dark blanket that stretched over the vale from side to side. A wide lake was the only patch of brightness. It lay glimmering deep at the bottom of the valley, still and smooth as glass.

Daisy tried to climb back on Thunder's shoulders, almost like she was scrambling up a tree. The big man grabbed her, pinning her frantic arms, and set her back on the stony slope.

"I cannot carry you here, little woman," he said urgently. "The way down is too steep. But take my hand until we are off the mountain."

Daisy clutched at Thunder's broad hand, and the moment his fist had engulfed hers, he set off down the trail, pulling her along. I followed, wishing he would go a little faster. But the trail down, if it can be called that, was doubtful, much more broken by rock and fir-tree, as if it had been even less used than the way up.

We had only gone a few steps when a sickly light was cast on the path before us. I chanced a quick look behind. The Deacon and his ghoulish nimbus were ascending over the rock seat like a ghastly green sunrise with a black core.

If I had wanted to go faster before, now I wanted to run right through Thunder, out into the backlands, and perhaps never stop. If the way had been any wider, I might have. As it was, I dodged back and forth behind his back, looking for any way through, feeling that dead gaze on my back, and expecting any moment the touch of a bony hand on my shoulder.

I was having a better time of it than Thunder, I think. He was having to hold himself almost backward to fight against the pull down the slope. I was lower to the ground. He was lean and wiry and tough, but he already seemed to be pushing against the limits of his endurance. Every now and then, he stumbled and almost toppled, and I feared that if he did go down, we'd have to leave him on the cold hillside at the Deacon's mercy, with all that would follow.

As we dodged boulder and brush, I was trying to think of something, of anything, that we might use against the Deacon. Pa had told us, in his time, lots of ghost stories and witch tales, and while he had never downplayed the scary dramatics, when the story was done, he had always emphasized, with special care, the remedies and tricks used to defeat the foes. I thought then that it was just to reassure us. Now, I ran over these ploys in my panicky mind as I fought my way down the mountain.

Fire sprang to mind. Fire was good for a whole set of reasons, being effective against warlocks or wild beasts. But I had run off without our tinder-box, and Thunder couldn't kindle his against the Deacon. Even if I took his, it was so time consuming, I wouldn't be able to strike a spark before the specter was upon us.

A Bible might have been useful, if we had one with us, either reading against the ghost or even merely as a talisman to ward him off. I hurriedly crossed it off the list as I stumbled over a particularly rough patch of stones.

Salt was supposed to be potent repellent for all evil spirits, whether demons, ghosts, or witches, especially if cast in a protective circle. Once more, I was stymied by our lack of supply. I thought yearningly of the salt box, resting comfortably on a shelf back in the cabin. Unless the lake down in the valley was salt water, that was the closest that factor lay.

The lake. Water! My heart rose. Evil couldn't cross running water! Doubt pricked my mind. Was the lake running water? I recalled its wide mirrored surface, and my heart sank. And if it somehow was, how could we put it between us and the

Deacon? If we ran around it, he'd follow, and we were far too exhausted to swim. I watched Daisy as Thunder had to drag her through dried, rattling brush and knew that.

I chanced a look back and almost ran into a tree. The Deacon was gliding effortlessly along our track, and the distance between us was closing. The only part of him that looked alive was his stringy hair, floating and fluttering in an unfelt breeze. Bats were circling his head, as if drawn to the glimmer of the unnatural flame he walked in.

My mind sped up as my legs tried to pump faster. Garlic. Rowan trees. Magic mirrors. If prayers could have stopped him, the Deacon would have dropped down like a door nail, for I was praying a mile a minute between thoughts. I was still praying when I suddenly realized we were off the mountain and running through a thinner patch of woods. The firs had turned to oak, maple, and hickory.

There were only a few scattered rocks, and little under-growth beneath the thick canopy of trees. It was darker, pierced here and there by slanting shafts of moonlight through the gnarled massive trees. I could finally run side by side with Thunder.

The Indian realized the situation the same time I did. Without missing a step or saying a word, he picked up Daisy and settled her under his arm, and trotted on, a little slower now. Thunder had swooped her up facing backward, and she cast a wild look at the Deacon, and then back at me, with a terror-stricken expression that only multiplied my own fear.

I thought about maybe getting ahead of Thunder, further away from the predatory corpse, and dismissed the thought. Even if I knew where we were supposed to be heading, I couldn't abandon them. With each step, the faint rattle of the money jar in Daisy's clothes reminded me that she was there and in my care. I wished he was carrying her the other way, so at least she wouldn't have to watch the abomination bearing down on us.

We ran on, through veils of shadow and moonlight that blinded us as we flashed through and back into the dark again. It was unsettling and nightmarish, as if the world had lost all stability, shifting uncontrollably from seen to unseen. In the dark stretches, I tried to judge the dim green light cast from behind us, to see if it was getting stronger, only to have it swallowed in the next bright beam.

So intent was I on escape that I had passed a clump of hemlock by a good nine yards before my mind registered the growl, and I probably wouldn't have stopped then if Daisy hadn't cried out. We slowly turned, the big Indian and I, to face a huge, grim, gray wolf, fur bristling and fangs bared, that had stepped out of the bushes behind us startled by our passage, poised to pounce.

A great stillness poured out of Thunder, and I caught it, as if by contagion. Daisy relaxed and stopped kicking her legs. Slowly, for a few seconds, the wolf was calming down, lowering its hackles and pricking up its ears. Then it whirled backwards with a growl, and its ears went flat on its skull. The Deacon was coming up behind it.

We watched, frozen. The black figure glided forward, neither slowing down nor speeding up, completely ignoring the beast before it. The wolf snapped and snarled, and even where I stood, I could see the whites of its eyes when it tossed back its head to howl. It grew ever more frantic as the undead wizard drew near but seemed unwilling to either attack or flee.

I dared to hope for a moment that the beast could actually

stop the revenant. It stood, its legs planted and tongue lolling, barking in defiance at the approaching specter.

The Deacon never even slowed. He held out a thin arm, his hand descending, gentle as a falling leaf, and touched the wolf's head.

"Shh," he said, one finger brushing within an inch of the foaming jaws.

The wolf dropped dead sideways to the forest floor without a sound or a quiver.

We stood stunned. The Deacon closed the space between us by another three paces before our wits snapped back. We turned and fled.

"Where?" I gasped. It was about all I could manage and still keep my breath as we loped along. Thunder didn't even try to speak but raised his free hand and pointed ahead. Far off beyond, and between the trees, I saw the glitter of water.

"Can't...swim," I wheezed. He said nothing but grabbed my arm and pulled me forward in a sudden burst of effort. I sensed this was a last desperate push. I could feel his arm muscles growing slacker as we ran, and as hard as we tried, we couldn't stretch the distance from our hunter by much.

As we ground on through the nightmare landscape, the lake ahead grew broader and broader until it looked like a shining wall blocking our way. I thought about the mortal effort it would take going around it, then started weighing the alternatives of slipping to my doom under its cold waters or awaiting the unholy touch of the Deacon's hand, with whatever eternal consequences that might bring. The still depths started to look mighty peaceful, almost welcoming.

I might have run right into it if Thunder hadn't pulled me back at the last second. We broke out of the trees abruptly, escaping the shadowy canopy of the woods. The sudden expanse of the moonlit, star-scattered sky, and the broad reflecting lake, bordered and upheld by mountains like clouds made solid, was overwhelming after the closeness of the stifling forest. I flinched for an instant before its majesty, as if it had just been created right before my eyes.

We were on the bank of the lake, by a small muddy beach fringed with rushes. On either side, hoary willows billowed drooping into the water, twining their branches amid innumerable floating fallen leaves and ancient jagged stumps sticking from the water. There was nowhere to go.

Thunder let Daisy slide wearily from his arm, and she landed on her feet with a squelch on the mud.

"What do we do now?" she asked, hopping from foot to foot, looking back at the green glow moving through the shadows behind us, going no faster but ever closer. "What do we do?"

"Give me a treasure, children." Thunder's voice was low and exhausted. I almost couldn't hear.

"What do you mean, a treasure!" said Daisy. "We don't have any treasure. I have Ma's money, but you're not getting that!"

Thunder shook his head.

"No, a treasure, something precious to you," he explained urgently. "Something that is only yours. We must make a gift to the lake before we touch its waters." His voice hardened. "Do it now!"

Daisy stared at him, then quickly undid the ribbon in her remaining pigtail and gave the thin blue strip to him. Her blonde hair hung down and poofed out, white as a dandelion clock in the moonlight.

I knew what that ribbon meant to her. It was the only gift she had from her friend, Theodora, to remember her by.

I quickly pulled out the contents of my pockets. There was my ugly worn old sling, two or three acorns, and the cheap brass-handled pocket knife that Pa had given me. I looked at the knife. I considered for a split-second the foolishness of throwing such a memento away, then weighed it against our imminent danger. I handed it over. The Indian deftly twisted the ribbon around its bow.

Thunder took our offerings and hastily pulled the pouch that hung under his shirt over his head, walking a way down the beach into the water as he did so. He stopped right in front of four long thin pointy stumps that stuck up out of gentle waves, the water black in the shade of the willows. He held up pouch and ribbon and knife in the cup of his hands and started talking.

It wasn't any language I knew, but I'd been to church enough times to know praying when I heard it, and begging praying, at that. I heard him say "Bob Bellamy" once. It's peculiar how you can always pick your name out of any speech, no matter how odd.

It couldn't have lasted long, but it seemed to go on forever as I looked back and forth between the beseeching figure of Thunder and the approaching dead glow of the Deacon.

Thunder stopped and spread his fingers, and the items fell with a *plop* into the water, echoed almost immediately with a *gloop*, like a fish had struck at them as they sank past the surface. This seemed to satisfy the Indian.

"They are accepted. Come, help me now!"

He clambered out of the mud and disappeared into an overhanging clump of willow, only to reappear tugging at the end of a battered heavy old canoe. So, this was why he had headed here! I sprang to his side and started helping him wrestle the unwieldy thing off the bank and onto the waves. Even Daisy tried to help, but when it was halfway free of the bank, Thunder picked her up and threw her in.

Her added weight and the water that it had shipped in at the seams made it tougher to wrestle the canoe through the drooping branches, but panic added a certain zest to our actions, for now we could clearly see the black core that was the Deacon walking in his nimbus of green flame. With a last almighty haul, the canoe broke free of the land and shot into the lake. I scrambled in, followed by the soaked and bedraggled Thunder and, for a moment, we rested, panting, while the impetus of the launch carried us forward.

I turned my head and looked back. The Deacon had reached the shore. Without a pause, he stepped onto the water and came straight toward us, as if he were walking over a field glassy with rain or a polished stone floor. Beneath him, the lake flickered, reflecting his witch-light and casting it back in a thousand broken fragments. Waves began to ring away from his path.

Thunder bent his head, his body sinking low. I thought it simply exhaustion, but he came back up holding paddles he had retrieved from the bottom of the canoe. His expression was grim.

"We must seek to live," he said. "A little longer."

He handed me a paddle. My hand almost sank with the weight of it. It had obviously been made for an adult with much greater strength and skill than I had. While I strove to get the oar in the water, Thunder was already pumping away, struggling to get the wallowing craft to move on water, which seemed heavy as syrup, and making little headway.

I made frantic digs at the black water, like I was trying to shovel up sand. I'm don't think it helped at all. I'd never been in any watercraft before, much less tried to propel one. Then one wild stab at the water yanked the paddle out of my hand and sent it flying away out of reach in our wake.

"Bobbie!" Daisy wailed in dismay. I slumped back down in the canoe. I was spent. I looked up at Thunder's broad back, still bowed at his rowing, each stroke slower and more agonized, until he stopped, too. Fighting legs that moved like lead, he turned and faced the fate that inexorably followed us, like blasphemy walking on the water.

The Deacon was almost upon us, maybe ten yards from the canoe. We were still gliding forward from our momentum, but even his dead steps were faster. The water under his feet was starting to boil, as if even the lake was disturbed at his presence, and it was sending ripples and waves across the otherwise calm surface of the water. The canoe started to bob and duck a bit, like it was bowing in submission to his approach.

It was close enough to see his face clearly. His eyes were milky in the moonlight, and his dead lips parted in a hungry smile that showed his yellowed crooked teeth. His moldy garments and flying hair stirred in that spectral wind that affected only him.

"Wait there," he rasped in a low voice that rattled in his throat but carried across the water. "I shall be with you soon." His smile widened to show the jagged dog-teeth and his black, withered gums.

Daisy tugged at Thunder's unresponsive arm, hopping in a frenzy, heedless of the rocking it caused.

"What do we do, Mr. Thunder? What do we do?"

"Wait," Thunder said impassively. He pointed a gaunt arm. "And watch."

So, this was it. All we could do was wait for the inevitable. I looked down yearningly at the cold waters and wondered if drowning was so bad. I looked up again, and then realized that Thunder was not pointing at the Deacon as he floated nearer but beyond, to the stretch of water between the wizard and the shore of the lake.

Something was moving there, under the water and casting up a wake.

It was hard to make out because it was shining with a pearly light that was masked by the frosty moon. If it hadn't been moving, and moving fast, I might have missed it. But a long, pale figure was undulating towards us and closing the gap with frightening speed.

I looked at the water and shuddered. It didn't seem so welcoming an alternative now. If it could harbor such unknown energetic monstrosities, I didn't want to embrace its depths anymore. The creature lifted its head and dipped back in. In that brief instant, I could see four horns sticking from its skull and a gaping, barbeled mouth.

"What is that!" Daisy shrieked, clamping onto Thunder even harder, kicking and trying to scramble up his body like a kitten up a tree.

"That is Onari, the Spirit of the Waters," said Thunder, voice calm and a little bleak.

"Is he going to attack us, too?" I asked.

"No, he has taken our tokens of passage. We begged him for his leave to cross." For the first time that night, a faint, genuine smile quivered around Thunder's lips. The creature, almost upon us, dove down, its pearlescent light vanishing into the abyss.

"But the Deacon has not."

The water boiled and exploded between us, and a long writhing white body leaped up and looped coil upon coil around the emerald-encased body of the undead warlock. At last, his unwavering pursuit was halted in its track, as he struggled against the attack of the thing from the lake.

I goggled at the beast. It looked like a cross between a snake and a colossal fish, covered with pale scales. It was hard to tell because it kept twining and curling, but it must have been at least twenty feet long. Its head was as big as a barrel, with a gaping mouth lined with needle teeth. Near the head were sharp, slashing fins that it raked against the Deacon's attacking hold.

For Whitley was attacking, trying to grasp the roiling body with his death grip. His hands kept slipping over the white sheen radiating from the creature's body. The light seemed to be acting like a shield. Onari was plainly not just some beast of the field that would fall to his touch. Whatever it was, it had power of its own. It tossed its horns in annoyance.

The Deacon, realizing his failure, switched tactics. He gathered his green fire into clusters in his fists. For a moment, they grew in intensity, then the flames shot out like lightning, raking the serpent body. At first, they glanced off, but as the wizard cast bolt after bolt, spots began to appear on the squirming scales, first bruised, then burned, then bloody.

Onari fought back, striking and snapping, attempting to find a hold through the Deacon's dark power. A fin struck the wizard's arm, and there was the *snap* of breaking bone that made me wince, but which didn't seem to pain Whitley at all. He redoubled his attacks, although a flick of the tail cracked a femur the next instant. He began a new tactic.

The Deacon started to rise. Slowly, foot by foot, he began to mount into the air, dragging the great beast dripping after him, its long body writhing in a furious attempt to hold onto the ascending revenant. Once it was hanging completely out of the lake, its light started to fade and the coils slowed down, starting to loosen.

"This is not good," Thunder muttered behind me. "Onari needs the power of the water."

I turned to him.

"Well, isn't there something we can do? Throw the paddle at him or something?"

"*I* can do nothing against him."

Suddenly, I heard the emphasis.

"But we can, you mean? That's why you led that old spook here! Somebody else can destroy him, but you can't!"

He said nothing, and a terrible thought struck me.

"But what about you? If Onari wins, will that kill you too?"

He sat impassive and crossed his arms. He wasn't going to help me with this. Maybe he couldn't.

But could anything help? Desperately, I went over the list of supernatural countermeasures in my head. Fire, salt, bells, bibles, garlic, running water…all around me the rippling water seemed to mock my wild speculation. The uncaring moonlight danced like silver on the waves.

Silver.

The pearly light was almost a glimmer now, shooting in erratic glints along the great serpent's body. Its coils drooped, and its staring eyes were filming over like a dead fish. I turned to Daisy.

"Quick, get out the money!"

"What! Why?"

"Never mind, I need a silver coin!"

"But Momma said…"

"Just do it!" I bellowed.

For the first time in her life, Daisy actually did what I told her. She fumbled the little bumblebee jar out of her tattered soggy dress, popped the lid, and scrabbled around, drawing up a silver dime that gleamed like a miniature moon in her fingers.

I snatched it away and stood up shakily in the canoe that wobbled nastily with the movement. I fought for balance while I reached into my pocket and brought out my tattered old sling.

I put the silver in the pouch and felt the weight of it. When I judged the canoe was as settled as it would ever be, I rocked the loaded launcher back and forth and started the whirl.

I got it going good and looked up just as the big snake fell bonelessly, exhausted, from the Deacon's triumphant green blaze. It tumbled with booming *slap* into the lake, wriggling off into the deeps. The warlock's gaze followed it into the darkness with mordant pride.

"Jerimoth Whitley!" I yelled.

His head snapped up at his name, and at the same instant, I let loose the reeling sling.

The coin smacked right into his forehead and sank from sight. He stiffened, head back, mouth gaping as if for breath, and howled. His green fire blazed up fiercely, then started to stutter and flutter. Slowly, he sank back down until the tips of his feet brushed the water. The ghostly wind he walked in ceased, and his green flame failed at last, but still he hung on the surface of the lake. He turned his baffled, snarling face right at me and tottered one step toward us.

The lake erupted again as Onari shot up under the staggering corpse, needle mouth agape, its battered but pearly light restored. It engulfed half the Deacon at once, and we watched in horror as his ragged arms struggled against the gullet and its rows of spiny inner teeth. With a *snap* and a gulp, the other half went down. Onari dove again, the long curve of its coils finally disappearing with a flick of its tail.

Thunder gasped, a huge intake of breath, and fell back into the bottom of the canoe. A tension had gone out of the air, noticeable only by its sudden absence, and I collapsed sitting, too. Daisy sprang up with a sharp cry and laid her head against the big man's chest.

It seemed an eternity before she lifted her head. My sight was going black around the edges.

"He's alive," she said.

"Good," I managed, then pitched forward into oblivion.

When I came to at last, Daisy was slapping me with her tiny open hands and sprinkling me with water. I reared up, sputtering and wiping my face. It was still dark, and the rocking told me we were still afloat.

"Good, you're awake," she said.

"Where are we? How's Thunder?" I sat up.

"I think he's all right, but I can't stir him. When that snake-fish thing went down, I guess its waves got us movin.'"

My eyes adjusted, and I looked around. The canoe was bumping amid the reeds that rattled in the night breeze. We had drifted right across the lake. We were cast up on the farther shore.

CHAPTER NINE:
A NIGHT IN THE BIG
WOODS

I sat all the way up, feet sloshing and skidding in the bottom of the canoe. It had shipped a lot more water and was awash to the waterline. If we hadn't nudged into shore, it would have gone down into the lake already. Thunder lay half-submerged in it, his iron-gray hair floating like water weeds around his head.

A night breeze started up, and I shuddered in the chill. I hugged my shoulders in a futile attempt for warmth.

"We've got to get out of this," I told Daisy, my jaws juddering. "Or we'll all be froze by morning."

"What about him?" she asked, gesturing at Thunder. "Do you think we can get him out?"

"We'll have to try."

For all his age and gaunt limbs, the Indian was solidly built, and his sodden clothes weighed him down worse. It was a hard lift for two wearied children, hollow with hunger, and one them barely off her leading strings. We managed to get his head out of the water and rested it on the rim of the canoe. We sat panting and recovering, while the vessel, rocked by our efforts, settled down. It was obvious we could never lift him out.

Daisy recovered her wits first. She had been watching where Thunder's head had been rolling to and fro with the movement of the canoe.

"Bob," she said, "We could rock him out."

"What do you mean?"

"Well, he's too heavy to lift, but this boat rocks with every little move. All we have to do is get it goin' and keep it movin' and, eventually, it'll overbalance and tip him out. Then we can slide him on up the shore."

I studied the idea for a moment. My brain was tired. I couldn't think it through, or come up with another idea. So, I agreed, reluctantly. What I really wanted to do was give up, crawl ashore, and collapse.

Instead, what I did was crawl over the side and land smack up to my waist in mud and water, which was somehow colder than the water in the canoe, though I couldn't have been much wetter. Daisy got out on the other side more carefully, never letting go of the hull.

"Now remember," I said, "when I pull down, you let up, and when I let up, you pull down."

"I know how to teeter-totter. Let's get goin'!" she said through chattering teeth.

We started to sway the canoe left and right. Cautiously at

first, until we caught the rhythm, and then we began to warm up. Thunder's unconscious body, which before had only rolled gently, began to pitch and lurch. Daisy drew in a great whoop of air every time her side of the canoe went up, and then she started to give a little defiant *yawp* every time she threw her weight into the down-pull. It got louder and louder each time until it was a screeching squawk, and then I found myself yawping back at her in an encouraging, escalating counterpoint.

We were so caught up in our effort that we were startled when it finally had the desired effect. The canoe suddenly spilled Thunder out into the lake and rocked violently back, sending Daisy flying off the other side. The rim grazed my chin and knocked me stunned onto my backside into the mud. I sat there dazed, shaking my head until I realized that Thunder was lying motionless, face-down in the reeds.

I tried to fumble my way toward him, my feet seeking for purchase in the oozing lake bottom. But before I could even get close, he exploded out of the water with a great gasp for air, hair dripping with water weeds, arms slipping and skidding as he fought his way up to breathe. He floundered his way onto the bank, threshing the water with each plunging step, at last flopping his way onto solid earth and collapsing, rolling over on his back into a convulsing, wheezing heap.

Daisy started striding through the reeds, up to shore.

"Well, that worked out all right," she said.

"We almost drowned him!"

"Pa says the only time that almost counts is in a game of horseshoes," she said practically and stepped up onto the bank. I slogged after her.

"Come on, help me get him up," I said.

Between us, we managed to haul Thunder forward by his arms into a sitting position. He was still heaving up water, and his bedraggled hair and drooping feathers dripped like rain into his lap. What worried me most, though, was his vacant stare. I held him up by both hands, and Daisy went behind and propped up his back.

I looked him hard, right in the eyes.

"Mr. Thunder," I said. "Mr. Thunder, where's your flint and steel? We need to make a fire.""

He gestured vaguely towards the lake.

"Gone," he coughed and shut his eyes.

That was that. No chance to strike a spark. If I had still had my knife, we might have found a stone and tinder, but I guessed Onari was probably at the bottom of the lake by now, picking bits of the Deacon out of his teeth with the blade.

"Dang," I said and looked at Daisy over his shoulder. "I suppose we'll just have to find a dry place to hunker down until the sun rises."

"No!"

The old Indian pushed us away and staggered to his feet.

"We cannot stay on this side of the valley," he croaked. "Whitley is gone, but the bindings we worked together are broken, and all will be awake and angry. We cannot linger. We cannot...stay..." His voice trailed away into a confusing jumble of English and Indian words. He took a few tottering steps forward.

"Easy there, Mr. Thunder," Daisy said, taking his hand to steady him. She turned to me.

"I think we better listen to him, Bob, and head on home."

I looked around and considered the damp bank and the wind shivering off the lake. I cast an eye over the long curve of the water, the tangled woods, and then up the ramparts of the mountain on the far side. I contemplated the forested miles between it and the cabin and thought how the moon was already on the wane. I drew a deep sigh.

"Well, I reckon we can start. At least the way back seems pretty plain. But if we find a good place, we're going to hole up and rest, no matter if all the spooks in the Territory are roused and running." I took Thunder's other hand. "Let's go."

We started off at a shuffling pace, kind of pulling Thunder along. For all his eagerness to leave, he didn't appear to have any clear idea where to go or quite what to do. I fancied the sudden relief from his run from the Deacon might have caused some collapse inside him. A sneaking voice in my head suggested that the snap of the spiritual cord between the two might also have something to do with it.

Daisy began talking, chattering along to encourage us on our way.

"Come on, Mr. Thunder, come on now. We're going on back home. Just follow my lead, and we'll get you over the ridge and back in more civilized lands for some breakfast, you'll see. You helped us, and we'll help you. Bob will find the way, you'll see. Do you want to hear a song? I know plenty of songs. Here's one Pa taught us. 'Ye sons of Columbia, who bravely have fought...' "

I won't tell everything she said, because after a while it got a bit repetitive, but it went on and on the whole trip. I got pretty irked with the stream of her babble, but I must admit the annoyance fueled my vexed spirits to keep going, if only so she'd be quiet at the end. It kept Thunder on his feet. If there was such a procedure as he told us of, I believe she did speak life into his weary body.

Where we had to go was obvious, but the way to get there wasn't so straightforward. If we could have kept the lake on our left and the mountain in front of us, it would have helped, except the minute we got under the trees we were walking in a maze, twisting, and turning to find our way past fallen trunks and impassable thickets. The shape of the mountain was lost in the shadows beyond. We couldn't see the placement of the moon or stars to guide us, though they shed a faint silvery light so we weren't in total darkness.

We trudged along, rattling up leaves as we went, Daisy's piping voice keeping counterpoint to the trilling of frogs and shrilling of crickets. Every now and then, there was a distant bird call, like mocking laughter, almost human sounding. At least, I hoped it was a bird. I didn't say anything, but I subtly steered us away from where ever it sounded like it was coming from. A mist started creeping along the ground.

Daisy noticed that Thunder's head had started to wag alarmingly and broke off a story she was telling about her friend Theodora. She patted his hand with vigorous little slaps.

"We used to sing a song, me and Thea. It was one of her favorites. It goes like this:

"My dear, do you know,
How a long time ago,
Two poor little children,
Whose names I don't know,
Were stolen away
On a fine summer's day,
And left in a wood,
As I've heard people say."

My head turned like it was on a rusty hinge, and I looked at her in disbelief.

"Daisy, do you have to sing that song now?" I creaked. She ignored me, or she didn't hear me, or maybe she was just too caught up with her recitation.

"...They on blackberries fed,
And strawberries red,
And when they were weary
'We'll go home,' they said."

Lucky beggars, I thought. I could use some berries right now. A whole bushful.

"That's enough, Daisy," I said aloud. She sang on, putting a little pathetic warble to it.

"And when it was night
So sad was their plight,
The sun it went down,
And the moon gave no light.
They sobbed and they sighed
And they bitterly cried,
And long before morning
They lay down and ..."

"Stop it!" I shouted. The trees rang with it.

Everything went silent. No birds, no frogs, no bugs, no Daisy. Thunder opened his eyes wide and stared at me.

"Let's get on," I said gruffly. Thunder squeezed my hand as if to calm me, and we shambled forward once more.

It wasn't long before Daisy started her monologue again. But she didn't argue about my behavior or finish that song, as I knew she would have at any other time.

"What do you fancy for breakfast, Mr. Thunder? If Ma got back with some flour, I'm thinkin' we could have biscuits and bacon gravy, but even oatmeal's soundin' pretty good right now, or a slice of toast with salty butter. But what I really fancy are some fresh eggs…"

My stomach squealed, and I wished she'd get off the subject, but I didn't rebuke her. We walked on.

As a matter of fact, we were getting bewildered. With all our detours and caution, we had lost sight of any guiding signs. I couldn't smell the lake anymore, much less see it. As the moon set, and the light we had grew dimmer, I paid more attention to how we were making our way.

"Oh, hell," I said. I stopped in my tracks, and Daisy and Thunder scuffled to a stop beside me.

"What?" said Daisy.

"I just noticed something. We've been taking easy low paths without thinking about it. We should be by the water or starting to climb by now." I tried to make my exhausted brain work.

"So?"

"So, I have no inkling where we are, and not the faintest idea which way we should go!"

We stood, Daisy and me, looking out at the vast woods, while all around us the pale moonlight was draining away. Thunder hunched between us, drawing shuddering breaths of cold night air, unable to walk, it seemed, unless we pulled him along.

Daisy tried to hug herself with one hand. Our clothes were still clingy and damp, and the mist oozing around our feet refused to allow us any warmth.

"What can we do?" she asked finally. "Let's keep movin', and hope for the best."

We lurched forward, dragging Thunder with us. He groaned with the movement but staggered on.

Just as the last of the moon failed, we stopped, stymied, in front of a crowded wall of weeds, tall as a man and with broad, interwoven leaves. I blinked. How long we had been walking since our pause, I don't know. Daisy's voice had faltered away to squeakiness, then silence. I looked to the left and saw a steep fall of stone. I looked to the right, and my dull eyes saw only a dense blockade of stalks, marching forever into shadow.

"Look!" Daisy cried suddenly, pointing. "There's a light!"

I shook my head. I saw nothing. And then I did. Deep in the tangled immensity, there was a flash of golden white light.

Impulsively, I took a step towards it. A sudden breeze sprang up, rattling and shushing the weeds, raising their leaves like forbidding hands. For a second, that checked me, then taking a firmer grip on my companions, I plunged us into the unknown, following the light.

For a moment it winked out, drowned in scratching, slapping leaves, then I saw it again, a little more to the right. I pulled us along in single file, Daisy dangling at the end and yelping at the swat of rebounding stalks. I threaded my way through, hurrying lest I lose it again. It appeared again to the left, and I corrected course. Then to my confusion there were two, then three, then dozens, and we came blundering out on the other side of the barricade.

They were fireflies. Hundreds of thousands of fireflies, more than I'd ever seen, winking and dancing all around us. It looked like the whole starry host of heaven had descended to earth to have a private shivaree . Their light was so strong, I could see our little group clearly for the first time for hours.

We were a sorry looking lot, standing like ghosts revealed in the trembling glimmer. Daisy's hair hung loose, tangled with leaves. Her dress was tattered and slimed and sagged with the weight of the bumble-bee jar still tucked in over the sash.

Her shoes were invisible, caked with mud up to her knees. Thunder held himself upright, but with an unnatural stiffness. His buckskins, tough as they were, were torn and filthy from his heedless progress. He gazed at the fireflies, jaw slack, dazzled by their dancing flame. I didn't dare look at myself. I could feel how wretched I was.

And to tell the truth, I didn't care. It didn't really matter how grubby I was. For a moment, I forgot that we were lost, and cold, and for a moment, I wasn't even hungry. I just stood in wonder at the beauty of the fireflies, dancing in their millions in the heart of nowhere, secret from all eyes except ours alone to bear witness.

"Aah," said Daisy, voice faint with reverence. Her hand had slipped from Thunder's arm.

I looked up. A tear was trickling down his cheek.

My own sight blurred. The radiant vision was becoming too overwhelming to bear. My head seemed to be chiming with each flash. I could just make out, past the firefly light, the dark shuffling shape of the woods. I bowed my head, grabbed Daisy and the old Indian, and fled crouching into the covering canopy.

The fireflies whirled in our passage, and a few trailed after us in the dark, only to flicker back to the flock as I stopped and watched, catching my breath. It felt like we had just escaped some danger. At a distance, the dancing light was merely earthly again. We watched it a while longer, and then moved on.

The forest was thinner here, and grew sparser as we went, so we could just see things by the faint sheen of stars. The shrilling of the crickets had died away, and we started to hear the shifting and sprinting of scurrying feet in the undergrowth, driven before our stumbling approach.

I was worried we might trip across something that would turn on us in the dark, when suddenly we dropped, thunder-startled, by the pounding of heavy wings just over our heads, riding on a fierce, hollow cry. We landed groveling in the leaves on the forest floor. A pale shadow had passed over us and struck the brush in front.

Trembling, I raised myself up on my elbows. Six feet in front of me was an enormous white owl, its claws stuck into something plump and furry, tearing off bits of it with its beak, and raising its goblin-eyed head with every bite to stare right at us.

I tried to get up and move back, and it roused its wings with a threatening screech. I froze. It settled and tore another gobbet from its kill. The blood sprayed out, glimmering black and wet in the dim light. Thunder stirred, then lay still, and when I saw Daisy trying to get up, I hushed her.

"Don't move," I said. The owl was easily as tall as she was.

I watched in bleak fascination as the gruesome bird feasted with grim deliberation. The violence and precision of its movements spoke of a desperate need, of tearing life out of death, and its threatening glance told me that I was myself caught up somewhere in that equation.

At last, it had its fill. With one final glare at us, it hunched, spread the full broad length of its wings, and sailed off into the night, the remains of its kill gripped tight in its iron talons.

I helped Daisy up and, together, we got Thunder to his feet.

"We better get away from here," I said. "No telling what beasts this blood could draw."

We straggled forward. I felt like we were not even trying to get anywhere anymore, but just pushed on by the impulse to keep moving. I could feel the bone in Thunder's arm like a frail stick, and Daisy's hand in my hand was a tiny glove filled with dice. The ground was starting to rise, and each step was a burning effort to raise my knee and put it down again.

I looked up, cold sweat streaming down my hair and into my face, and saw a dark ridge like a wave, rising, bumped with hunched shapes against the night sky. At last, I thought. A high place. If we get there, we could look down and see… What? Where we are. A way to go. A place to rest. Anything.

"Come on," I said hoarsely. "A little way more."

We began clambering upward, grabbing shoots and saplings and rocky outcrops, whatever we could pull ourselves up by. The top was growing nigh, and I was getting delirious with expectancy

"Get up," I kept saying, yanking Thunder's coat. "Get on up. Little ways more. Get on up."

We struggled up to the brink, bruised and battered with the climb, and I stretched out a triumphant arm to grasp what looked like a huddled mass of rock. It exploded upward with a roar and stood towering against the stars. I had put my hand on a bear.

I felt my innards melt, then freeze. The brute stood, tall, terrible, and archaic, as if he had just been born out of the rock he stood on. He looked down on us, judging, grunting, snorting the air. I felt that any minute he would topple down and tear us apart with his heavy claws, and that, somehow, in his majesty, that it would be right. This was his domain, and we were trespassers, a blot on his sovereignty. I felt strangely calm, humbled under his immense power, and waited for the blow to fall.

"Peace, brother." Thunder's voice came, scarcely louder

that dry leaves rustling in the wind. I slid my eyes over to him. He slowly withdrew his arm from my hand and put his fist over his heart.

"Peace, brother," he breathed. "There is no harm in us. We are lost and passing through your land. Peace, brother. There is no war between your blood and ours."

The bear started to relax, as if it were listening to his words, but it kept staring down on us fixedly. Slowly, by degrees, he went down on all fours, but his gaze never wavered. Finally, he turned, dismissing us as of little consequence, and rambled off along the rocky outcrop, heading into the uplands.

I waited till the beast was well gone, then let out a deep sigh. Without a word, I climbed to the top of the ridge and looked down.

My heart broke. It was another valley, tangled, trackless, almost barren, a shallow cup in the circling hills, full of broken monolithic stones and dead trees. Thunder and Daisy came up behind me. The old Indian put his hand on my shoulder.

"I know this place," he said bleakly. "This is the Land of the Old Ones. This is as deep into the Forbidden Heart as one can go. And as far from your home as we can be." He shook his head wearily. "We have been led here, I think."

"The Old Ones," said Daisy. "Are they still here? Can they help us, or will they hurt us?"

"They are long gone. My people drove out the people who drove them out, years ago. These stones are all that is left of their houses."

"Houses, huh? Can we shelter there?" I asked.

"I would not. They are *a-ta-ken*, holy and horrible."

I shivered. The night wind was keening off the mountain. I made a decision.

"Well, we're going to. If we been led here as you say, then these Powers you talk about meant us to be here, and there's nothing we can do about it. And I, for one, am too blamed-tired to do anything else." I squared myself off and marched down toward the rocks. Daisy scrambled after me.

"Bob! What are you doing?"

"I'm going to find a crack out of the wind, hunker down, and give myself up to whatever happens next."

She put her hand in mine.

"Sounds good."

We were joined the next moment by Thunder. He looked ready to drop, but for the first time since the lake, he seemed clear and collected.

"I think you are right, Bob Bellamy. Let us find a place to rest at last."

We wove our way across the sandy bottom, through the toppling spires of stone. If they had ever been parts of a building, weather and age had long since worn them down into misshapen blocks. We finally found a place where two titanic slabs made a sort of corner. Leaning against the place where they met was the tattered stock of a tree, thick and more than twice as tall as a man. It was covered in what looked like peeling, spongy bark. The wind broke itself against the stones, and here in their lee, we cast ourselves down at the foot of the stump and leaned back, eyes shut in exhaustion.

Thunder passed out almost immediately, hardly surprising considering our trials. But, somehow, his abdication made it difficult for me to surrender right away, like someone still needed to keep watch. Daisy was snoring lightly on the other side of him, snuggled up for warmth. My eyes shut on their own, then jerked open when I felt myself slipping away, only to begin drooping once more. My eyes popped open again, to see the old Indian's unconscious body being drawn up soundlessly and stealthily from between us.

I was too scared to move or raise my head. Then two long, hairy arms furled down from above and silently scooped us up.

I screamed then, and that woke Daisy, and she screamed too, short, sharp screams, one after the other. I felt myself lifted through the air with frightening speed, and then held dangling in the air. I looked, and saw I was under the scrutiny of an enormous, inhuman face.

What I had thought a tree was a lumbering creature, shaped most like a man, but wild and uncouth, and covered from head to foot with long, trailing hair. The only places I could see bare were parts of the face and the palms of hands. If he had feet, they were invisible under shambling tendrils that scuffled the debris at the end of his trunklike legs as he looked quizzically back and forth at my sister and me. Thunder had been slung over his massive shoulder like a skinned rabbit.

He gave Daisy a little shake, and she stopped screaming, the wind knocked out of her for a moment. Slowly and carefully, he tucked us close to his body, almost cradling, and began striding away from the rocks.

I struggled and squirmed, beating against his furry hide like a drum. I might as well have been punching a sack of sand and iron bars, for all the effect it was having. I kept trying to twist free, then looked down at the rocky ground passing by, ten feet below me. I decided discretion was the better part of valor, and went still.

"Bob," said Daisy, catching her breath back. "Where do you think it's takin' us? Do you think it has a castle?" She tried to move her arms, and when she couldn't, tried to bite. She spat out a mouthful of hair. "Giants eat people, Bob!"

"It ain't no giant, Daisy! That's just fairy tales." Even now, I was trying to be rational. "It's… Well, it must be some kind of monkey if it ain't a man."

"Well, that's real comfortin'!" she wailed. "You know what baboons eat, Bob? Meat, that's what!"

"Pshaw," I said. "It's not acting hungry. In fact, it's acting like we're its babies. Settle down, and let's see what happens."

"All right, but if there's a stewpot at the end of this trail, I'm holdin' you responsible!"

As a matter of fact, I was starting to feel warm and comfy against all that fur, and the rocking motion of his wide, sure-footed pace was lulling me to sleep. I looked into his face as the unseen branches went whooshing by in his wake and saw what I thought was sad wisdom in his liquid eyes. Somewhere along that late-night dream voyage through the trees, I fell asleep.

When I woke up, we were still striding along. For all his bulk, the creature was stepping as delicately as a deer, almost noiseless. I could tell the sun was about to rise, and a few early morning birds were sending out cautious practice calls. In the light, I could see that his fur was gray-green, and his eyes deep brown under his craggy brow. I glanced around. The woods we were passing through were less dense, and somehow familiar. When we went by the fallen chestnut oak, I suddenly knew where we were.

"Daisy!" I hissed. "Daisy, wake up!"

She blinked herself awake, and before she could scream again at our gigantic captor, I whispered hoarsely, "Look! He's taking us home!"

She goggled around at the woods.

"Are you sure?"

"Yes. Look, there's the stream!"

His swift steps had indeed brought us to within sight of the purling water. There was the arm of the hill that hugged the cabin, and over that hill rose a plume of blue smoke.

The beast took us right up to the edge of the stream but seemed unwilling to cross the boundary of its water. He unfurled his arms, set us gently to the ground, then took Thunder carefully in both hands and almost tenderly set down him down on a bed of moss. Then he did something that surprised me most of all.

He looked me and Daisy in the eyes, shook his head, and put one long finger to his lips, as if enjoining us to silence. My eyes went wide. He smiled a little, turned, and went pacing off in that mile-eating gait. In a short time, he was lost in the misty trees and the rising sun.

Daisy and I crossed the stream and walked around the corner, where a babble of voices contended in the clear, morning air.

Chapter Ten:
Lost And Found

We approached the sound with caution, pausing before we turned the corner. These were voices I had never heard before, and the memory of yesterday's raid—had it only been one day?—made me wary. Then, rising above the hubbub, I heard Ma's cry, sharp and loud.

"We must begin at once. Can't you see? The sun has risen at last. We are wasting time. We must get on the trail."

Another voice, and this time I recognized Mr. Culpepper.

"Let the men finish, Mrs. Bellamy. This might be their only meal before nightfall. Remember, they're here for your assistance. Don't grudge them five minutes to prepare for the day's labor."

"I begrudge every second while my children are in danger, sir. I thank you all that you are here to help, but I beg you, let us start. I will not rest until I find— My babies!"

The last words were shrieked in a tone I had never heard before. At the first sound of her voice, Daisy and I had started hurrying around the hill, and just then we had stepped into her sight. We paused, momentarily confused.

Ma was standing among a dozen people unknown to us, some mountainy men in outlandish furs, others townsfolk in simple work clothes, all carrying some type of a gun. They were surrounded by their milling horses. Ma herself looked wild and unfamiliar, eyes red and hair half put up, armed only with the walking stick I had cut for her, looking ready to thrash the world until it yielded up her children. But she cast the stick aside as she raced forward, swooped, and, despite our filthy appearance, clamped us into a hug that promised to never end. Not that we wanted it to.

When it did, we found ourselves surrounded by puzzled faces, some smiling, some not. One trapper, whose beard and hair seemed to grow twining down into the varied pelts he was wearing, scowled and spat.

"Woman," he said. "I'm tetched you've got your young'uns back, but where the tarnation have they been? I don't want to've lost half-a-day of trapping for a couple of runaways spending a night camping in the woods."

Daisy struggled out of Ma's embrace and turned on our accuser, shaking her finger up at his face. She looked like a baby chick threatening an old hound dog.

"Well, you can set your mind at rest, mister, 'cause I was kidnapped by the MacCallister Gang, and Bob here followed them to rescue me."

There was a burst of deep incredulous guffaws all around. Mr. Culpepper, at the front of the encircling men, didn't laugh, but looked doubtful, squinting. Ma stood up, held me at arm's-length, and searched my eyes.

"Tell me what happened, Robert."

I hung my head. I twisted my dirty, tattered shirt-tails and looked down at the toes of my broken shoes.

"It's true, Ma. I left Daisy alone to go foraging, and when I came back, they were running off with her. I took out Pa's gun and went after them."

"Where's the gun now, Robert?"

"I lost it, Ma." I looked up. Her eyes were gentle but searching. I straightened up and set my shoulders back. Time to face up to it. "To get Daisy back, I challenged Captain MacCallister to a duel. I shot him, then dropped the rifle when we ran away."

Stunned silence, then another explosion of disbelieving laughter.

"The boy's a hero!"

"My mother 'ud a tanned my hide if I tole her a lie like that!"

"Never heard such a whopper!"

Ma went on evenly, cutting through the scoffs.

"And then what happened, Robert?"

Every time she said my name, I felt a little tightening around my heart. I resolved to simply tell her the truth, but not yet the whole truth in front of this group of skeptics.

"We ran away—the wrong way—until Mr. Thunder found us. We wandered around with him a bit, and then we all came home."

"Oh, yes," Daisy broke in. "Mr. Thunder's on the other side of the spring, and he's in bad shape. We've got to help him, Ma. He saved us, he really did."

"That lazy old savage?" The furry trapper spat again. "Probably wanted to score a handout."

"Quiet, O'Brien." Culpepper was stern.

Daisy blushed red and turned on the mountain man in fury.

"What do you know about it, you old yahoo? Nobody's askin' your opinion, anyhow! Mr. Thunder is a good man and our friend! You're so eager to get back huntin', why don't you go catch a skunk?"

O'Brien snarled, turned on his heel and stalked off. I think he saw there was no good end to exchanging backchat with a six-year-old child.

"Thank you for coming to help, Mr. O'Brien," Ma called politely, but absently, after his retreating back.

"Bah!" he said. He found his horse, swung into the saddle, and rode off under a sour, sulking cloud.

"Some of you men, help me get old Thunder over here," Culpepper ordered. Nobody noticed. They were still watching Ma as she was closely examining me. They were expecting a disciplinary spectacle, it seems, for having made them gather to no purpose. At last, she nodded.

"I believe you, Bob. I want to hear all there is about it, later." She looked up at the ring of incredulous faces.

"Robert is an honest boy." She turned smiling to me.

"It's good to have you back, son."

There was muttering among the rescue party at that, but Culpepper took the opportunity to re-assert his authority.

"You heard me," the old veteran commanded, thumping his cane on the ground. "Jehu, Abner, let's get Thunder over here and have a look at him."

"I would say you should," said a scrawny old lady, pushing

her way to the forefront, her sun bonnet flouncing with each step. "Leave it to a bunch of men to stand around jawing and judging while a pair of waifs are ready to drop starving, and a poor charitable heathen laying in the woods in a bad way. Get a move on!"

The circle broke before her like abashed schoolchildren, and Mr. Culpepper collected a couple of burly townsmen to go with him to the stream.

"Thank'ee, Clara," he said in a lowered voice before he went and winked at the lady. She flapped her apron at him to shoo him along, then gathered us up under her wings.

"Come away, my darlings. Come and have some breakfast. I think these great fellows may have left a little in the pot."

"Children, this is Mrs. Culpepper. She volunteered to accompany her husband, to feed the searchers and help wherever needed. Mrs. Culpepper, Robert and Daisy, my prodigals."

I nodded my head bashfully, but Daisy went all the way and paused to bob a curtsy. The formal gesture, performed so gracefully despite her ragged appearance, charmed the old lady no end.

"Come, come, you must eat," she said, her smile breaking through a mass of wrinkles, her eyes buried in the folds twinkling black like crickets. She herded us into the cabin, to the hearth in the parlor. A black cook pot sat by the fire, and a short fat man stood in the corner. He had clearly decided that the excitement was over, retired to the kitchen, and with wooden bowl and spoon, was busily scooping up another helping while the getting was good.

"Tully, I think you have had enough now. I hope you saved something for these poor urchins."

Unashamedly, the man put the bowl down and took up his hat.

"Very fine dish, Mrs. Culpepper," he said, covering his head. "My compliments." He sailed out of the room.

I looked at the bowl. It was scraped clean.

"Ach," the old lady said, lifting the lid on the pot. "We are lucky, the kind man has left us some. Sit at the table, children, and I think you, also, should eat now, Mrs. Bellamy. She said she wouldn't, you know, until her little ones were found. Don't stir. I shall serve you myself."

I helped Daisy into her seat, then hopped up into the other chair. Ma hovered near, like she'd never let us out of her sight again. Mrs. Culpepper got some fresh bowls and clean spoons out of a square wooden kit and ladled out steaming yellowy-brown portions of some sort of unknown provender.

"Eat slowly and with care," she said. "Your stomach must catch up, first."

It was a kind of meat porridge, made up mostly of ham and cornmeal and black pepper. After a few eager mouthfuls, Daisy asked what it was called, and the old lady answered with a double-jointed Dutch word we couldn't wrap our tongues around, no matter how often she repeated it.

"I think I have a new favorite breakfast," Daisy said. Later, Ma got the recipe, and though she ended up making it for us many meals thereafter, I don't recall it ever tasting so good as it did on that chilly morning after our night of peril.

Once the edge of hunger was off, Daisy raised her head and reached a hand down her blouse. With a clank she fetched out the little tin jar and handed it over to our wondering mother. Parts of the cheap gilded paint were worn away, and there was already a hint of incipient rust in the moldings.

"That was gettin' mighty uncomfortable," she declared. "It's mostly all there, but I do owe you a silver dime. That was Bob's fault, though."

"Indeed? Would you like to tell me about it?"

"I'd much rather hear about what happened to you yesterday," I said hurriedly, holding out my bowl to the old lady. "And may I have some more porkmeal, please?"

Mrs. Culpepper was much amused by my improvised nickname and took my dish to fill it up, but I don't think Ma was fooled for an instant by my diversion. Nevertheless, as I tucked into my second helping, she told her tale.

"When I took the road back to Cumberton, I found the straight trail down the mountain on the second bend, and so made good time, arriving back at Culpepper's Trading Post a little after noon. He was surprised to see me so soon, and when I had described our misfortune, we bartered a deal where he agreed to take back the ruined flour for a small abatement on the full price of another sack. Once more Mr. Culpepper kindly offered me a ride up the mountain, to cart the new flour back to the cabin and to fetch back the old bag for use as pig-feed.

"We got back to the cabin late in the afternoon to a scene of desolation: door open, our belongings looted, and both of you vanished." She paused.

"I hope I never experience such a thing again. You are my most precious things in the world, and after your father disappeared... Well, I was ready to run off after you right there and then. Mr. Culpepper was able to restrain me only with some force, and then with some harsh reasoning.

"He pointed out the lateness of the hour, the apparent size of the raiding party judging by their tracks, and my paucity of firepower. He voiced his suspicions that this raid could very well be the work of the notorious MacCallister Gang, known to be in the area. He proposed he go back to town, raise a rescue party, and return with it at dawn's first light.

"I reluctantly agreed, seeing the sense of his plan, and told him that I would remain at the cabin and light a beacon fire, in case you could see it and make your way home in the night. Mr. Culpepper started back to Cumberton, and I sat up to watch.

"I waited a terrible stretch of hours. At times I was tempted to grab a brand from the fire and rush headlong into the forest, to run calling your names in the off-chance that I might find you in the vast wilderness of the night. Sometimes, I thought I should sleep, the fresher to start the chase in the morning. Only I couldn't. A tense brooding wouldn't let me rest. When I peered searching into the shadowed woods, I felt that something was looking back.

"About midnight, the tension broke. Sudden calm settled on me. I had finally accepted, I suppose, that there was nothing to be done until morning. I piled more wood on the bonfire to keep it going as long as possible, wrapped myself up in a blanket by the cabin door, commended us all to Providence, and fell asleep."

I made some quick calculations. By my reckoning, that would have been just about the time the Deacon went down to his watery end.

"I awoke an hour before sunrise, guilty for letting myself sleep and seething with fresh anger at whoever had taken you. I paced in and out of the cabin, doing anything to distract me and speed the time. When Mr. Culpepper came rolling in with a dozen volunteers in tow, I wanted to start at once but had to stand champing at the bit while Mrs. Culpepper prepared a quick meal to fuel the hunt. They were still eating when the light finally fully broke, and I was urging them to start the search when you appeared around the corner."

She smiled again, happier than I had seen her smile in many a day.

"And here we are, together again, my darlings."

Mr. Culpepper came thumping into the room, leaning heavily on his walking stick, sweeping his hat off as he entered.

"Ladies," he said. "We got Thunder over the stream in a litter, and he's parked outside now. He looks to be fine, apart from a few scrapes and bruises, but he won't wake up for anything. Just plain exhausted, I figure." He looked sideways at me.

"It must have been a rough night."

"Yes, sir," I said. "It truly was."

He raised his eyebrows at my laconic answer, and when he saw no more was forthcoming, addressed Ma, forging ahead.

"Anyways, as there's nothing more for them to do, I'm going to dismiss the boys and thought you and your children would like to thank them before they go. In the event, they didn't have to do much, but they certainly showed willing, and it's best to keep that attitude cultivated among your neighbors."

"Indeed, Mr. Culpepper. Robert, Daisy, come here."

We hopped down, and she spent a moment doing what she could to spruce us up, brushing off mud and tugging our clothes into place. She took out a comb and raked it through our tangles with more or less satisfactory results, then put her own hair up again with more care. If we had had any fresh clothes, we would have changed, but the MacCallister gang had cleared us out.

"There. We're as pretty as we're going to get, I think," she announced. "Let's go, Mr. Culpepper."

He bowed her out with his old tricorne hat, indicating that she take the lead. His wife waved cheerfully at us as we filed from the room and started to clear away the dishes.

Outside, they had leaned the makeshift litter they had constructed of rough-cut poles and old blankets against the cabin wall. I turned to look at it as we passed. Thunder was bundled up inside it, only his face showing, eyes shut and mouth drawn. Daisy made a brief move to go over to check on him, but a firm directing push and a gentle shake of Ma's head indicated other duties came first.

Mr. Culpepper took a stance by his wagon, where the volunteers were gathered, taking swigs from a barrel on the back. We drew up beside him, me and Daisy on either side of Ma. The old man cleared his throat for attention.

"Well, neighbors," he began, "As all things seem to have come to an unexpected but fortunate conclusion, I guess we can go on home and be about our business. But before we disperse, Mrs. Bellamy would like to address you all. Mrs. Bellamy."

Ma stood a little taller.

"Good friends and kind gentlemen…" she began but was interrupted by the appearance of a horseman, galloping up the road in haste, black tailcoats flapping. The crowd scattered aside to let him in, and he pulled his gray horse right up in front of Mr. Culpepper and flung himself to the ground. He was dressed in black from head to foot, except for a white cockade on his hat and a badge like an eight-rayed sunburst on his lapel.

"Sorry I'm late, Amos," he said breathlessly. "Hope you weren't waiting on me. Bit of a to-do down at the depot."

"Nothing too bad, I hope. Anyways, the kids turned up on their own, only a little worse for wear. So, what was the ruction, Constable?"

"Only good news," he said, accepting a proffered drink from the crowd. He took a couple of swigs between puffing gasps. "That rogue MacCallister's been shot, and he and his gang caught when they tried taking him to a doctor in Burghley." Another swig. "By tunket, I wouldn't mind being the man who got him. There's a reward for actions leading to his capture."

A short man in shirtsleeves, with a head of porcupine hair, jumped forward and grabbed my hand in his calloused grip.

"We got the feller right here!" he crowed, yanking my arm into the air. "He was tellin' us about it even afore you came!"

"It's true! He was!"

"Well, I'm blessed! You should be mighty proud, Mrs. Bellamy!"

"The boy's a hero!"

The mob surged in, suddenly eager to congratulate me with this astonishing confirmation of my story. I stood speechless as they jostled me with their backslaps and shook my hands numb. I nearly cried with relief. I hadn't killed a man, after all.

Well, least-ways not one who wasn't already dead.

"Here, give the law room!" The constable pushed his way to the front of the crowd. "Some quiet there!" Up close and beside his dark clothes, his head looked like a stern but kindly brick.

"Now then, lad, tell me what happened, and don't spare the particulars."

I retold the story of the duel, and everything I could recall about the gang, particularly Captain MacCallister. This time, the audience was hanging on my every word, and the constable nodded as I went on, apparently checking details off a mental list. I concluded with an abbreviated version of the journey home. I was already pushing the more wondrous elements of the night into the corners of my mind, out of sight.

"That all sounds correct, as far as it goes. Tell me, do you think you could lead us to this campsite?"

"I think so, sir."

"Very well." He looked up at Culpepper. "Amos, I'd like to deputize you and a couple of likely men to find and examine the *corpus delicti*, as it were."

"I though you said he weren't killed," said the porcupine man, puzzled.

"It means the evidence, not the corpse, you ignoramus," the constable said loftily. "Don't let's bring him, Amos."

Daisy, who had been hanging in the background quietly up to now, came elbowing her way through a forest of knees, to stood indignantly before the officer of the law.

"Before anybody goes anywhere, somebody got to move Thunder inside. You can't just leave him propped up like a log against the wall. He's got to be where we can look after him."

Eyebrows were raised, and before anything was said, Ma came up behind her and laid her hand's on Daisy's shoulders.

"My daughter is right," she said firmly. "That man brought my children back to me, and we will nurse him until he is well again."

Looks of consternation, while I could see the idea of an Indian, no matter how elderly and debilitated, left unguarded in a cabin with a lone and lovely woman, playing through their heads.

Their speculation was shattered by Mrs. Culpepper, who had come out to see what the commotion was. She shoved her way through the gawping men to plant herself at my mother's side.

"What are you standing here for?" she scolded. "You heard Mrs. Bellamy! You know Thunder! Bring him inside, and we will tend him, and maybe when you get back, you won't have to dig a grave, yes?"

"You're quite right, dear heart," said Culpepper, shaking himself and blowing out his mustache, as if to clear his head. "Abner, Jehu, you're elected again. Why? Because I can trust you, that's why. Move Thunder in and set him where the ladies tell you. Then you're deputized for this little trip."

He turned to the volunteers.

"My Clara will see things done right here. The rest of you boys might as well clear on off home. Who knows?" he asked, poker-faced, "maybe you'll be the first one back with the news."

The thought sank in, then there was a scrambling avalanche of feet and a cannonade of hooves, and before the brawny deputies had even reached Thunder, the yard was cleared. The two men toted him inside and laid him down as directed in the hall, next to the fireplace.

A fire was kindled, on the general principle that a chill was to be avoided at all cost, and as I turned to leave the little house, the ladies were raising his head onto a bolster to make him more comfortable. Daisy sat next to him, holding his blunt hand and talking to him in a low, soothing, pattering stream.

I reached up and kissed Ma.

"I'll be back soon," I whispered.

She looked at me wildly for a second at the thought of separation again so soon, then accepted it, and let me go with a squeeze of her hand. I left the house and joined the men.

Outside, already mounted, were the constable, Mr. Culpepper, and Abner and Jehu, who were introduced to me as Cumberton's blacksmith and carpenter, respectively. There were two horses for each of them and one for me. Luckily, I had more experience in riding than in driving and was able to get on my horse without any humiliation.

I looked around and with a little difficulty was able to find the tree with the broken branch. The season had taken another turn to fall overnight, and the other branches were fading to the same color as the dead one. I pointed out my landmark, and we set off.

It was quite a different experience this time, riding with companions in the growing daylight. It might have been confusing, but the way seemed burned into my bones now, and I led us from place to place, pausing and dismounting now and then to study the trail. The constable got down and examined the tracks once or twice himself.

"Looks consistent with a large group of horses," he grunted. "Lead on!"

The trail started to rise, and when I found the three-way path on the hillside, I knew exactly where we were. We took the low road, the horses choosing their steps as slowly and carefully as mountain goats. Then we trotted through the trees and underbrush and came the clearing where the duel had taken place.

The first thing on entering, my horse's hooves kicked something metallic in the grass. I jumped down and came up triumphant, holding the object for all the see.

"My Pa's rifle!"

The others got down and gathered to see. The constable took it, felt the weight, turned it in his hands, snapped it open, then held it up to his nose and sniffed.

"Well, it's been fired," he pronounced. He handed it back and pointed to the camp. "Let's take a look over there."

We tramped over to the fire pit, our approach chasing off a couple of raccoons scavenging among the ashes. I looked in disbelief. There were scraps of the marauders' soup and the overturned pot laying around. If I had walked into an old abandoned villa in Rome and found a gladiator's feast still warm on the table, I don't think I would have felt more disoriented, so much had happened since the duel. The men walked around, examining the scattered debris.

"Yep, these are the Bellamy's things all right," said Mr. Culpepper, rocking a small barrel of baking powder under his boot. "I sold them this just two days ago. Right, Bob?"

"Oh, yes, sir," I said, hurrying to his side. I looked around at our tumbled goods spread willy-nilly in the scrub grass and thought of the winter ahead.

"Mr. Constable, can we get all this together and take it back with us?"

"In good time, young man. Right now, let's look around a little more." He grinned. "And my name's Hearn, Mr. Bob. Constable is just my office."

"Come look at this!" It was the carpenter. We gathered round, and he pointed down at a great patch of flattened weeds. In the middle was a blotch of blood, sticky and dark with buzzing flies.

"And over there!" A trampled path led off east. The

constable held his arm up and sighted along its length, considering.

"Going that way will get you to Burghley," he conceded. "Why don't you fellows gather these things up. Bob, let's you and me walk the perimeter once."

I tried to keep pace at his side as we made a circle around the clearing.

"This is the tree where Sugar held Daisy," I said. He examined it briefly, and we walked on. "And about here is where I turned and fired."

"Hm. You drop the gun?"

"No, I pretty much flung it away. I didn't see where it landed."

"Until today." He saw something and walked into the bushes. "Some tracks here. You ever go in here?"

"No, sir."

"See any of the gang go in here?"

"No."

"A minor mystery then." He emerged again. "Oh, well. Maybe one of them relieved himself before you ever got on the scene." He brushed his black coat. We walked on.

"I have good news for you, lad," he said, as we drew close to our starting point. The others were finishing up loading the horses with our recovered belongings. "From everything I can find, your story holds true. When we get back, I'm going to write up my report, get Mr. Culpepper and these lads to sign it as witnesses, and send it in with my recommendation that you get the reward. You have any idea how much it is?" he asked, eyes sliding over to me.

"No, I don't, sir."

We paced on, each step punctuating his next words.

"One. Hundred. Dollars."

My head reeled. One hundred dollars would see us comfortably through the winter, with a very merry Christmas to boot. I could feel a grin starting to spread across my face that threatened to squeeze my eyes out. Mr. Hearn looked up casually at the sky.

"And I'm even going to overlook, just this one time, the fact that dueling is highly illegal and punishable under the law. After all, you were in very trying circumstances. But please, don't make a habit of it."

My face fell. I was sober as a judge the whole trip back.

Chapter Eleven: Fame And Fortune

We arrived back at the cabin in the late afternoon, the retreating sun shooting parting shafts of scarlet against the encroaching night. The rising wind was plucking a few gilded leaves from the wood, a foretaste of the wholesale plunder to come. Under the advancing shadow of the mountain, the lights of the cabin looked homely and harboring.

Thunder was sitting up in his improvised bunk, Daisy by his side, who was trying to press another spoonful of gruel past his clenched jaw.

"Come on, let's finish the bowl."

He spoke only through his lips, teeth clamped against the watery gray oats.

"I tell you, little woman, I have had enough."

The ladies had peeled him of out of his clothes. His

buckskins hung stretched out and pegged to the wall, washed and mended and drying, and he looked to be dressed in an improvised nightgown, stitched together from old sheets. Mr. Culpepper cackled at the sight.

"Thunder, you old pagan, good to see you're alive! Take care now, and you might live to be a hundred yet!"

The Indian cast me a beseeching look as I passed. I could only give him a grimacing smile of empathy and a shrug and leave him for the moment to Daisy's tender care as we trooped into the parlor to report.

It was a bit of a squash to get in, and when we did, it was hotter than blazes. Constable Hearn instantly sent the deputies back out so there could be more room to breathe, but even so, we were roasting after the cool evening air. Ma and Mrs. Culpepper were brewing a soup from Ma's turkey, which had been hanging quietly unremarked in the cupboard all this time, and was now simmering with potatoes and onions from the emergency supplies on the Culpepper wagon. A huge slab of cornbread lay baking in the ashes, glowing like a gold ingot.

The constable's report was acknowledged with enthusiasm, but of even more instant importance was the return of the supplies which, to Ma's joy, included our clothes. Daisy and I were ordered to an instant bath and a change into fresh things, and sent scurrying down to the stream with a cake of recovered soap. We took turns dipping in, eyes averted for privacy.

"You didn't talk to anybody about the Deacon or the water snake or the giant, did you?" I asked eventually, as we dressed. The clean clothes felt comfortingly assuring, reasserting the everyday mundanity of things.

"'Course not," said Daisy. "I don't want people to think I'm a loony. But we will tell Ma, won't we, when we get a chance?" She tied the pink sash of her Sunday dress.

"Sure," I said. I was quiet, thinking. I pulled on my good pair of shoes. "Sure."

We returned to a feast. Our bundles had been unloaded and stowed, and the horses pegged at a distance. A trestle table from the wagon was laid out in the yard, lanterns had been lit, and a cloth spread. On the table was rich thick turkey soup, swimming with dumplings and taters, hot cornbread and salty butter, and a variety of pies that Mrs. Culpepper had brought along for the volunteers.

There was the keg of small beer, too, to wash it all down. I was allowed a mug in celebration, and as the meal progressed, I was toasted several times. Daisy had to be content with some sour apple juice.

As ladies and the founders of the feast, Ma and Mrs. Culpepper were granted the two chairs from the parlor. The rest of us stood. Thunder, as an invalid, remained lying in the house. I don't know if it was ever considered inviting him out. Daisy would travel back and forth to the cabin every now and then with a sliver of turkey on cornbread or a slice of pie and returned looking pleased when he accepted it.

The stars were twinkling when Constable Hearn announced it was time to head back to town, and the blacksmith and carpenter agreed. Food and furniture were packed away. Mr. Culpepper said that he and Clara would stay the night and sent back word for his shop-boy to take care of things till they returned. The three men said their farewells, the carpenter promising to come back soon to see to the roof, and set off down the road. The rest of us retired into the cabin for the night.

The old Indian was already asleep. It was agreed the ladies

would bundle up in the parlor, and that Mr. Culpepper and I would bivouac with Thunder in the hall. After making ourselves pallets on the floor as comfortable as possible, including blocks of wood wrapped in blankets for pillows, we settled down. Full, tired, and satisfied, in a short while, I was slumbering deep.

I woke up sometime in the small hours. There had been a noise, I knew. Its absence rang in my ears. I looked to my left where Mr. Culpepper lay. He was snoring, but in a low, steady drone. Thunder's bunk was a silent lump to my right. I raised my eyes, and in the faint glow of the crawling embers saw a vast, shapeless shadow by the door, stealthy arms creeping along the wall, exploring.

I breathed in something sharpish, and the figure turned toward me quickly. Gleaming eyes and craggy nose highlighted by the dim fire dwindled the apparition into Thunder, draped in his bulky bed-garment. He had buckskins in hand, picked from the wall.

"What—" I began.

He held up a warning finger, then pointed to the door. I got up as quietly as I could, wrapping my patchwork blanket around me and grabbing my shoes as I rose. My slight shuffling sounded raucous next to the noiseless movements of the old Indian as he lifted the door and pushed it open just enough for us to slide through, and then he eased it shut.

Outside, the grass was frosty and seemed even more so in the bright moon, which was only now starting the road down from its peak. I slipped my shoes on and drew the blanket tighter as Thunder stepped into his leggings, then billowed out of the gown, hung it by the door, and drew on the fringed jacket.

He seemed to re-assume his dignity along with his natural clothes. It came to me that he had been diminished in the company of the townsfolk. Now, he stood like a gray monolith in the moonlight. The image of the bear flashed briefly in my memory.

"What are you doing?" I asked, whispering. We started moving a little farther from the cabin's entrance, and as we went, I dared speak a little louder. "Is something wrong?"

"No, it is very good. For the first time in many nights, I can walk without fear. And now I shall go. I must thank you, Bob Bellamy. Your mind was quick and your hand strong, even when Onari's power failed."

I was glad right then for the washed-out colors of the night, because I felt my face going very hot and I was afraid I was blushing.

"We wouldn't have gotten away if we'd met the Deacon without you," I said. "Or got by after."

"Nor would I, if you had not been there. You both have done very well, you and your sister. I do not think you need worry about Them if you wander in the woods now. You have been looked over and accepted." He started to walk into the trees. I followed, leaves crackling underfoot.

"Will you be all right?" I asked. I felt reluctant to part. I wanted to say a lot of things, about my gratitude, and my respect, and my regret. "Do you need anything? Food? Fire? Tools? I'm sure Ma would give you anything you want."

"I have caches here and there, which hold all that I need. Thank your mother for her care, and say farewell to your sister for me. It will be hard for her, I think. I shall come back, but now there are pardons to ask, and angers to soothe, and pacts to settle once more."

I don't want to say he grinned, but there was the shade of one playing around his impassive face.

"And I must leave before these white women tend me right into the ground." We turned back to the path, looking ahead.

We halted, brought up short. The leaves scuttered to a silence. We stood in front of Deacon Whitley's tomb.

Only, it wasn't a tomb anymore. An errant ray of cold light stabbing through the gloomy canopy of trees showed that it had collapsed into a tumbled heap of loose, broken rock. The little horn window lay cracked and empty at its foot.

We gazed at it solemnly, and I felt a sneaking, smug satisfaction. The hills were free. Whitley's power was broken, and I had a big hand in that.

Then something inside the pile *clinked*. My blood went cold. Thunder stiffened. A few shards clattered down, the rocks stirred, and something dark started oozing out of a space in their middle.

Then it waddled out onto the heap. It was a big, sleepy woodchuck, rolling with fat. It paused, wary of our presence for a moment, then squatted and took a loud, long water on the Deacon's grave. It scurried off into the underbrush.

"Well, I guess we can take it that that is that," I said. My voice shook, but whether from laughter or relief, I myself couldn't tell. I knew I was ready to go back to bed, and that it was time to part ways. I put out my hand to the tall, gaunt man.

"Goodbye till we meet again, Thunder. Take care of yourself."

He put his hand on my shoulder and looked me deep in the eye.

"Bob Bellamy, my name is Thunder-That-Calls-From-The-Mountain."

He went striding off into the moon-streaked woods.

The next morning, Daisy was upset with Thunder's unexpected departure, and was only mollified when I explained things and said that he had promised to return. Mr. Culpepper, when he learned Thunder was gone, wasn't surprised.

"Never did know an Indian that would stay under a roof longer than he had to."

There appearing to be no more need of nurse or chaperone, the Culpeppers packed up their wagon and bid us a fond adieu. After a flurry of handshakes and hugs, supplied mostly by Daisy, our family stood waving as the old couple rattled around the bend, and then it was just us again, in the clearing in the woods.

But we weren't alone long. Right before noon, after we had cleaned up from yesterday's affairs and were finishing our chores, a trickle of people came threading up the hillside. It never really stopped over the next few days. It was folks wanting to congratulate us, me in particular, and to hear me tell the tale.

The men came for the gruesome details, and to shake the hand that had brought down the notorious Captain MacCallister. The ladies came to offer tributes in baked goods, and to point me out to their own sons as a shining example of bravery. The boys were kind of wary of me, and I felt I probably wasn't making any friends there. Some looked in envy, some in awe, at the boy who had shot a man and got a reward for it. As for the girls, they were another thing altogether.

They flocked on me, like fish on bait. Ma had thrown my old clothes from the adventure into the rag bin, and I had to go around in my second-best. Not Sunday best, you understand, but still better than every day, and my hair had been cut and combed, my nails trimmed. A local hero, not positively ugly, and with a handsome reward coming in, was a powerful draw, I reckon.

They swarmed around Daisy, too, petting her and cooing over her imagined hardships, telling her how lucky she was to have a brave brother to come to her rescue. And under the influence of this attitude, each time I told the story, Daisy was relegated deeper and deeper into the part of the damsel in distress. She sat there and seethed, ears burning fiery red.

I had to tell the story, again and again, and eventually told it at the Captain's trial. Now's a good a time as any to recount how that turned out. He was found guilty, of course, and spent the next twenty years as a celebrity in prison, where he wrote his book. I imagine young idiots are still reading it and forming romantic ideals about thievery.

His wife was let off by a sympathetic jury. She opened a boarding house near the prison and used much of the proceeds to make MacCallister's life in jail as comfortable as possible. With the help of our testimony and recommendation, Sugar was freed, and he went on to settle in the area and brought his family over. Grisly Joe was sentenced for five years as an accessory, and when he got out, he promptly disappeared, heading west, they said. It's hard to imagine he had a peaceful end.

Billy Straw was declared incompetent and daft as a loon. He was advertised, with descriptions, but no one ever came forward to claim him. The old man ended up working for Mr. Culpepper in the stables and spent his remaining days happily tending to, and living with, his beloved horses.

When the third day had gone by, I still hadn't told Ma

about the more uncanny elements of our lost night. The time never seemed right, and she didn't press things, though she knew there must be more. Maybe she was unwilling to hear it, suspicious of what it might be. Maybe she was waiting on me.

The longer it went, the harder it was to bring up. Daisy was eager to tell, but not if I wasn't ready to begin. Afraid to be thought a little baby story teller, she said.

The morning of the fourth day dawned, and I couldn't take it anymore. First thing at breakfast, before I thought we would be beset by any more sightseers, I opened my mouth.

"Ma," I began, only to be instantly interrupted by vigorous rapping at the cabin door. The house echoed with it.

"This is getting ridiculous," Ma said, throwing down her napkin and rising. "We shall have to post visiting hours, at this rate." I got up and followed her, annoyed but curious to see who could be calling at this hour of the day.

She flung the door open, then stepped back, eyes wide.

"Mr. Frobisher!"

The lawyer stood there, sleek and solid and dressed to the nines. In that rustic setting, with his laced hat and long riding cloak and fancy walking stick, he looked like a peacock in a hen yard.

"Mrs. Bellamy," he replied, doffing his hat in a quick, businesslike manner.

"Forgive me for asking, sir, but what are you doing way out here?"

"Well, as local officer, I was out riding the law circuit… May I come in? Thank you. When I heard about young Bob's exploits… Hello, young man. And as I had intended to check in on you while I was in the area anyway, I took it as my duty to collect the reward and deliver it to you right away. And here it is." He patted his breast pocket, then reached in and drew out a neat packet.

"One hundred dollars, Bob, in crisp new banknotes." His wattles shook with a wry chuckle. "You're lucky the prize was put up by the local bank. If it had been the government, it might have been a long time coming."

I took the fat envelope gingerly, not even daring to open it. It wasn't as satisfying as the sack of gold coins I had been imagining, but the thought of all that wealth contained inside radiated awe.

Daisy cocked an eyebrow. She had heard me tell her about Frobisher.

"Count it, Bob," she said flatly.

Frobisher laughed indulgently, and Ma glossed politely right over it.

"Thank you for taking such troubles for our family. Would you care to eat with us?"

"No, I have already breakfasted in town, but perhaps a cup of that coffee I smell before I go?"

"Certainly."

Ma breezed into the parlor with as much grace as if she were in silk instead of gingham. Before he followed, the old lawyer bent down to me for a private word.

"Well," he asked, "did you ever find Whitley's lost treasure?"

I had forgotten about that illusory hare he had started so long ago in his office. That idea certainly seemed unnecessary now. I thought about the beauty of the valley, the wonder and terror of the mountains, the friendship and valor of Thunder.

"Yes," I said. "Yes, we found the fortune he lost."

Frobisher looked puzzled, but Ma said the coffee was ready, and he left me and Daisy alone in the hall and went in to more practical matters.

"Well, don't just stare at it, open it, mush-head," said Daisy.

I put my thumb under the red wax seal and broke it. The envelope crackled open, and there lay twenty fresh, five-dollar banknotes, covered in fancy swirls and art, and the ink barely dry on the treasurer's signature. They looked almost too pretty to touch, but I counted them three times before I was satisfied.

"It's all here," I said.

"Good, now count out at least half of it and set it aside for Thunder."

"What! Why?"

"'Cause though he wouldn't say it, I know it was Thunder shot Mr. MacCallister, not you."

I stared at her.

"What in jabbering botheration are you talking about, Daisy?"

"Thunder shot him, not you. You were wobblin' all over the place. Thunder came up out of the bushes and shot from behind you."

"Well, I didn't see anything!"

"Well, I did! I couldn't see his face because of the hat, but he was wearin' his buckskins."

"Hat! When was he ever wearing a hat?"

"He must have lost it, after."

"And what about a gun?"

"What about it? You dropped yours, too! He was probably 'fraid he'd get in trouble for shootin' a man. Who knew there was a reward?"

"Thunder did not shoot MacCallister, I did!"

"Did not!"

"Did so!"

"Here now, children, what's all this quarrel?"

We turned at the sound of the stern voice. There in the entrance stood a man, who had opened the door unnoticed while we were fighting. A man with straggling long hair and a bush of a beard. A man in a slouch hat, and fringed buckskins, leaning on a tall rifle. Daisy and I stopped, struck dumb at his appearance.

"What's going on—" Ma began, as she came out of the parlor, then caught sight of the man.

"Chase!" she cried and flung herself on him. His hat fell off backward under the assault.

"Elizabeth!"

I gawked. It was Pa. Skinnier, hairier, more tanned than I remembered, but it was Pa. He was alive.

Mr. Frobisher, coming out after Ma, stood in wonder at the reunion, and when the kissing didn't seem likely to ever stop, cleared his throat.

"Mr. Bellamy," he said, looking at him over his square spectacles. "Mr. Bellamy, I am gratified to see that you are still in the land of the living, but do you mind telling me please where in the world you have been?"

"You're not my Pa," Daisy announced.

"Whoa," said Pa, letting go of Ma and ignoring Frobisher. He bent down to the defiant girl. "Daisy Paulina Bellamy, of course I'm your father. Look at me. Don't you remember me?"

"'Course I remember my Pa." she said. She crossed her arms. "He was taller and didn't have a beard."

"Well, you have grown a sight, since we last saw each other," he said, and grinned.

"It's been over a year, Chase," said Ma. That was the closest I ever heard her come to reprimanding him about it.

"Far too long," he agreed. "What do you say you bob my ears, and I'll scrape my chin, so our daughter can recognize her long lost father? And is that breakfast I smell?"

So back we went to the parlor and sat down to breakfast once again. Pa ate ravenously while Ma hunted out his shaving kit and whipped up a lather in his old mug. As he started scraping off his beard by the reflection in the coffee pot, he told us his story, with one eye cocked at Mr. Frobisher, who sat, hands folded on his walking stick, chin on chest.

"Well, to begin with, that mission you sent me on went a lot further and took me a lot longer than you guessed, Frobisher. All the way to New Orleans, in fact. But that's for later. When I finally got back to report, you were gone on circuit, and then I found that my family had moved out of the city. Their land-lady told me they had headed for Cumberton, so I decided first things first, and I'd find you later.

"I turned up in town five days ago and was directed to this cabin. I hurried up that twisty road, but when I got here, the place was ransacked, and nobody here, and a beaten path heading into the wild."

"We must have just kept missing each other!" said Ma. "I took the straight path down."

"That sounds like the confounded luck I was having. I found a marker pointing the way—"

"That was me, Pa," I said. He nodded.

"I headed out after it, but night fell, and I wandered a bit. I was getting desperate when I caught sight of a campfire, and

I crawled cautiously up to outside the light, just as that duel was coming to a head. To my horror, I saw you, gun wobbling all over the place, and MacCallister drawing a steady-handed bead. I popped up quick behind you and winged the rascal."

"Oh."

He must have seen how crestfallen I felt. He patted my back.

"It was still plenty brave, son, and I don't think we ever need to reveal the details, do we, Frobisher? The money's still in the family, after all."

"Indeed not, Mr. Bellamy. In fact, considering your, ah… occupation, it would be preferable you kept a low profile."

"That's fine with me. So, when that crazy man doused the fire, I lost you two again in the shadows and the steam and the gunsmoke. I ran a little way, then realized I'd lose the track in the dark. I had to sit till the sun rose before I could trail you again." He finished shaving and set the razor down.

"We were home by then."

"I didn't know it. I had to cast around a bit, and finally knew I was on the right trail when I found this." He reached into his pocket and pulled out a strip of blue.

"My other ribbon!" said Daisy. She grabbed it from his hand and started tying it around the end of her ponytail. "At least I have one to remember Thea now. Thanks, mister."

Pa looked exasperated.

"Can we start that trim now, Elizabeth?"

Ma tucked a towel around his neck and brought out her kitchen scissors and a comb. As delicately as she could, she began snipping.

"So, I tracked you all the way over the mountain, and lost you again at the lake's edge. I fetched a long way 'round the shore until I struck your trail again, and then it weaved and wandered around like a drunkard. I saw, of course, that there was somebody with you, and wondered if he was leading you astray— Damnation, woman, that's my ear!"

"Language. Sorry, dear." She pressed the towel against the nick till it stopped bleeding.

"I followed that trail into the greatest maelstrom of supernatural power I've ever met, in all my years in the Bureau of Shadows."

"Mr. Bellamy!" Frobisher jumped to his feet. His jowls quivered. "Must I remind you of your oath of secrecy?"

"After what they've been through, I owe my children the truth. I'd say they can handle it."

Ma sighed.

"I thought it must be something like that, mixed in this business. I never wanted them to know. It's so…unnatural, and it stains the soul. You know it does, Chase."

"What's the Bureau of Shadows, Pa?" I asked.

"It's the Department of Extranatural Affairs, Bob, a government agency established to investigate reports of ghosts and monsters and witches. Nobody's supposed to know about it. It goes against the official policy of Enlightenment. But we're here to guard the spiritual health of the nation."

"Which we can't do if people go around blabbing about it," the old lawyer grumbled, settling back into his seat. He gestured grudgingly. "Continue, Mr. Bellamy."

"I was caught for a day and a night, trapped in some caves by a … Well, maybe there *are* some things I'd rather not tell. I only escaped with the help of an old medicine man called Thunder."

"Mr. Thunder!" Daisy squeaked.

"That's right. When he got me out, he told me everything you kids had gone through, and everything you had faced. A revenant, Frobisher, and a lake monster, and a forest giant. In one night! He told me you kids were home safe and set me on the right road back. And here I am."

"I must apologize," Frobisher began. "If I had thought it was anything other than perhaps a spook…"

Ma's scissors went still, and she pulled the towel out, scattering tufts of hair.

"All done!" she said, revealing his new-shorn head. Pa turned.

"Pa! It is you!" Daisy jumped into his lap and buried her head in his chest, wiping her suddenly weeping face back and forth on his shirt.

Pa held her gently.

"I told you it was, Daisy dear." He looked up at the lawyer.

"So, what do you think, Frobisher? I'd say Bob here would make a pretty good agent."

"To replace you when you get suspended for this. Do you have your report?"

Pa's hand dove into his coat pocket and took out an oilskin pouch.

"Here," he said. "A pretty bedtime story for the president." He threw it flopping to the table and reached into another pocket.

"And Bob, I heard you lost your knife. Take mine. I've been thinking to get a new one, anyway."

It was heavy iron dagger, sheathed, about a foot long, with a horn handle. I pulled it out and studied it. There were some strange symbols carved along the blade. I recognized the All-Seeing Eye.

"That's not made for ordinary work, but it answers for most common needs. Take good care of it, and it'll take care of you."

"I will, Pa." I pushed it back into the sheath and stuck it through my belt. I felt about ten feet tall.

"Don't you think you'll need that?" asked the lawyer.

"No, because now I'm going to take some recovery time for a few months and actually be with my family. I think, with a bit of fixing up, this place will make a snug, private little retreat for the winter. And I think I've earned it."

Frobisher sighed.

"Yes, I suppose you have. Upon review…"—he picked up the oilskin—"I'll see about sending the rest of your pay along. Perhaps while you're here, you can look further into this *maelstrom* of yours. But I warn you, come spring, there might be another mission for you."

He stood up and turned to me.

"And for you, too, perhaps."

He bowed to Mother.

"I see my prophecy has come true, madam. No ghosts or redskins have overcome your family. In fact, your fortunes have worked out very well. And so, until we meet again." He bowed and left, shutting the door behind him. After a moment, we heard the jingle of his coach driving off.

Pa looked around at us.

"So," he said. "What do we want to do first?"

That's my peculiar adventure, and that's how it ended. If there's one thing I've learned, it's that it's not just blood that makes a family, it's what you go through together and the stories you tell. And now I've told my story to you

About The Author

Bryan Babel was born in the Southwest Texas town of Seguin. In 1975, at eleven years old, he read *The Hobbit* and the road went ever on from there. *A Grave on Deacon's Peak* began as an actual dream he had two decades ago, and tinkered with on and off. It just wouldn't let him be. He shares his little house with two thousand books or so, an aging cat, and a miraculously refilling jug of sun-brewed tea.

CPSIA information can be obtained
at www.ICGtesting.com
Printed in the USA
FSHW021956091119
63843FS

9 781951 138011